P9-DXG-320

A New Universal History Of Infamy

A New Universal History Of Infamy

Rhys Hughes

The Ministry of Whimsy Press
Tallahassee, Florida
2004

MINISTRY OF WHIMSY PRESS
www.ministryofwhimsy.com

Ministry Editorial Offices:
POB 4248
Tallahassee, FL 32315 USA
ministryofwhimsy@yahoo.com

Ministry of Whimsy Press is an imprint of:
Night Shade Books:
3623 SW Baird Street
Portland, OR 97219
www.nightshadebooks.com

Cover Design by John Coulthart
Interior Design by Juha Lindroos

Editor: Mike Simanoff (mike@simanoff.net)

British spellings have been retained to
preserve the author's original intent.

Set in Sabon

ABOUT THE MINISTRY OF WHIMSY
Founded in 1984 by Jeff VanderMeer, the Ministry of Whimsy takes its name from the ironic double-speak of Orwell's novel. The Ministry is committed to promoting high quality fantastical, surreal, and experimental literature. In 1997, the Ministry published the Philip K. Dick Award-winning The Troika. In more recent years, its flagship anthology series, Leviathan, has been a finalist for the Philip K. Dick Award, the World Fantasy Award, and the British Fantasy Award.

Trade Hardcover ISBN: 1-892389-83-5
Limited Edition ISBN: 1-892389-84-3

I dedicate this book to Eber Marcela Soler: Argentinian, astonishing and an angel. Also: I offer her my smiles, winks and kisses, all of them touched by time, but for the better. Thirdly I renounce irony where it interferes with sentiment unfairly and denounce sediment where it clogs rivers unhelpfully. Besos!

AMOROSA ANTICIPACION

Ni la intimidad de tu frente clara como una fiesta
ni la privanza de tu cuerpo, aún misterioso y tácito y de niña,
ni la sucesión de tu vida situándose en palabras o silencios
serán favor tan misterioso
como mirar tu sueño implicado
en la vigilia de mis brazos.
Virgen milagrosamente otra vez por la virtud absolutoria del sueño,
quieta y resplandeciente como una dicha que la memoria elige,
me darás esa orilla de tu vida que tú misma no tienes.
Arrojado a quietud,
divisaré esa playa última de tu ser
y te veré por vez primera, quizá,
como Dios ha de verte,
desbaratada la ficción del Tiempo,
sin el amor, sin mí.

JORGE LUIS BORGES, *Luna de enfrente*

Table of Contents

INTRODUCTION
BY JOHN CLUTE

It is still early days to square the 1000 circles of Rhys Hughes. It is still too soon, in other words, to attempt to understand any one Hughes story, or cycle of stories, in terms of the whole. For many writers, of course—especially those who make no claim to understand what it is they are going to do with their lives, who abjure any sense that the stories they unfold are part of a superordinate project—the issue does not really arise: each story strives to utter itself as art, each tale a unique phial which, accessed in solitude, in the perfect silence of understanding, proves sui generis. This is not Rhys Hughes's goal. He has declared his intention to write precisely 1000 stories (altogether, in his life?), and to link each separate story backwards and forwards to every single one of its mates. Something like a 100 of these stories have been published so far; many more, it is understood, have been drafted. Links are indeed visible—characters and venues and Shapes of Story appear and reappear—but clearly we cannot yet really guess if Hughes's ambition to become the Balzac of the Fractal is clown hubris or something that will manifest itself, strange and magnificent and extremely huge, at the heart of our understanding of the landscape of the fantastic.

We can say this, though: that what is visible so far grows, like Antonio Gaudi's cotton candy Barcelona cathedral, like a bejewelled toadskin, like Cthulhu, in the mind's eye; and that each story seems hot to the touch of the mind's eye on the page, because *nothing can be what it seems*. Everything Rhys Hughes has written and published so far *vibrates* to musics we are not really sure we are yet meant to hear, or recognize. Those musics we do hear are mostly echoes, parodies, plays upon, homages to other writers (though what we sometimes think of as an echo of the prior may be a premonition of a yet-to-be-released story by Hughes himself). The effect of all this is dizzying (Michael Moorcock is on record as saying Rhys Hughes seems to have read everybody), for it is dizzying not to know whose tune we're dancing to, or have overheard, or (as I said a minute ago) are not really meant to hear yet. Each story constitutes a rumour that it is legion.

Which means that the stories of Rhys Hughes to date cannot really be read, usefully, like fascicles in a dictionary not yet completed: because the alphabet of the whole will not stay still, the alphabet is daily growing, and anyway some of it is Greek (to me). It is certainly not the case that Rhys Hughes has read everybody—he has not, for instance (personal communication), ever run across J B Morton (1893-1979), who published a lot of books under his own name, but who was better known for the comic column he wrote as "Beachcomber" for the London *Daily Express* from 1924 to 1975. This column, full of surreally intermittent narratives, spoofs and parodies and japes, and featuring characters like Dr Strabismus (whom God defend) and Captain Foulenough, comprehensively underlies much of 20th century British humour; much of it remains uncollected, though volumes like *Mr Thake* (coll 1929), *Sideways Through Borneo* (coll 1937), *A Bonfire of Weeds* (coll 1939) and the posthumous *Cram Me With Eels* (coll 1994) do sample the trove (just as, in another tense, proleptically, what Hughes has published so far samples *his* trove). For half a century he was inescapable, and in that sense anonymous. Through his obvious influence upon the great Spike Milligan, who himself clearly subtends many of Hughes's effects—and upon the less significant but very funny Maurice Richardson, whose *Exploits of Englebrecht: Abstracted from the Chronicles of the Surrealist Sportsman's Club* (coll 1950) strongly affected Moorcock, and subsequently Hughes—Beachcomber is a kind of Boojum beneath the antic terpsichoreum of joke and join we are beginning to look at here.

Beachcomber and Milligan and Richardson and Moorcock and Hughes don't get mentioned in one sentence exactly by accident: what links them, beyond a diminishing vein of outright humour, is a sense they convey that the world is a vaudeville; that the landscapes of the world are props to be yanked aside and changed at the drop of a hat or a halo; that the people who inhabit—who dance across—this stage are mimes; and that it matters little if the stories they act out are stolen, or borrowed, or new, or blue, because what matters is that the show (the 1000 stories yet to make their appearance) must go on. Protagonists, venues, plots are gear. The show is the thing.

There are of course other influences, further japes, deeper homages: other figures who contribute to the echolalia include Edgar Allan Poe, M R James, William Hope Hodgson ("The World Beyond the Stairwell" is perhaps the finest parody-with-love of Hodgson ever written), E H Visiak (maybe), H P Lovecraft, Franz Kafka, Dylan Thomas, Ray Bradbury (an upended radioactive version), Italo Calvino, Milorad Pavic (whose Khazar is a country that does *turns*), Monty Python, John Sladek (for the oulipo-like games, and for the searching, zany, radical humour), and lots more. These figures—and I think there are a *lot* more who could be listed—have appeared in stories published in magazines of very considerable invisibility, and, until recently, in volumes equally shy. But *Eyelidiad* (1996), a short novel, still surfaces, as does *Rawhead and Bloody Bones and Elusive Plato* (coll 1998), two novellas. More recently, four collections have appeared: *The Smell of Telescopes* (coll 2000); *Stories from a Lost Anthology* (coll 2002); *Journeys Beyond Advice* (coll 2002); and *Nowhere Near Milkwood* (coll 2002), which expands vastly upon a short collection with the same name from 1997. It is just now getting possible to begin to suss Rhys Hughes. (One of these days I may sit up in my tub like Archimedes, and say: Hey, I think I get it! Every story is every story! It's all *arithmetic*!) And there is, of course, one influence I've left out of the lists above.

Jorge Luis Borges.

2.

We need to come at this from a couple of angles, before we sign off on what Rhys Hughes has done here, in this book in our hands at this moment, *A New Universal History of Infamy*, which is a collection of fake biographies and other fictions constructed as a direct take-off from Jorge Luis Borges's *Historia universal de la infamia* (coll 1935; translated by Norman Thomas di Giovanni as *A Universal History of Infamy* 1972; later translated by Andrew Hurley as *A Universal History of Iniquity* in his version of the *Collected Fictions* 1998, which assembles all of Borges's fictional prose); Hughes takes the di Giovanni title rather than the Hurley, probably because the former wears the sanction of time, and sounds better (though "iniquity" may fit the case of the stories it describes better than "infamy").

First we need to get some sense of the iteration of Borges which has inspired in Rhys Hughes a desire to do something that—it would seem—cannot be done, to write a book in strict imitation of a book whose author copied everything he could grasp from books and world into words that seemed prior to their source, and who wrote in imitation of nobody. And then, it might be an idea to try to convey some small sense of the text these words forward, this *New Universal History of Infamy* which purports to reiterate without anxiety—at some points sentence by sentence—the second most famous title generated by a writer who did not himself seem to have precursors; an author whose influence on others, just like Franz Kafka's, seems to lie fathoms beneath the language in which it is uttered.

Certainly it seems clear enough that the *Historia universal* lacks any clear precursor. Not only do the crystalline deadpan fake-histories that make up its bulk have no precedents in the literature of Latin America, but the most famous single tale in the book, "Hombre de la esquina rosada" (which di Giovanni renders as "Streetcorner Man" and Hurley as "Man on Pink Corner"), was the first explicit fiction Borges ever published (1933 in Crítica): so not only does *Historia universal* start off part of Latin American literature, it also (in a sense relevant to us) starts Borges. To be influenced by the Jorge Luis Borges of 1933 is, therefore, precisely not to be *like* Jorge Luis Borges. We can go too far in proclaiming his originality, the sui generis aura that braces even his most explicitly parodic or derivative or problematically fictional pieces, not to speak of the clear clarion note of *newness*, seemingly out of vacuum, that marks every page of *Historia universal*; we can go to far, but not too far too far. . . Before Borges, we must remember, there was no Borges; and in pretending to map "Streetcorner Man" through the turns and twists of the story he calls "Streetcorner Mouse," Hughes is pretending to do what he knows cannot be done. Nor, in the event, does he make any attempt to disguise the profound difference between Borges's tale and his own, some of whose sentences, some of whose minute grammar, exactly maps its model.

"Streetcorner Man" is a tale much thought about by lovers of Borges, partly through its magical neatness of construction (the tale of a murder, which takes place out of sight, as narrated by a man who never tells us it was he who committed the crime; it's as neat as Agatha Christie); but perhaps mainly because it represents Borges's effort to incarnate himself deep inside a mythos of Argentina, a streetwise, macho, gaucho, criminalized version of the innards of Argentinian life which he could not himself have greeted in the real or physical world. From "Streetcorner Man" to "Streetcorner Mouse" is some leap, therefore, requiring a certain chutzpah; and it is a relief to recognize how successful the trip has been. Hughes makes no attempt to replicate the labyrinth of exile at the heart of the gaze of the true author of "Streetcorner Man"; we are in Wales, in a venue—a pub called The Tall Story, where Hughes has frequently used for the telling of Club Stories; and we are in the company of previously encountered folk like Tin Dylan, a monstrous (and maybe monstrously bad) pub singer who is not human.

His confrontation with Llygoden, the dominant male in the invaded pub, and the playing out of the drama between these two, and the narrator, and the woman Bronwen, maps Borges's tale intimately, except for the comic metamorphoses undertaken by the cast; and except for the fact that the implied author of the tale—Hughes—instinctively casts his tale as though it were part of a *conversazione*, which of course it is. It is not only that "Streetcorner Mouse" is part of the 1000 tales due to

bite our tails like Escher. It is also that the solitude of Borges's early 20th century attempt to assimilate the raw data of a longed-for history is here transformed into a talk- and icon-filled early 21st century Breakfast in the Ruins. Which is how, we may guess, Hughes thinks history has come out. There is no raw left; there is no vacuum to make sound out of. "Streetcorner Mouse" is, in this sense, a tale of mourning, a farewell to Borges addressed to the moment in time and space of his becoming Borges. Its loudness is a body English of all the histories since 1933. The fact that this central act of severance from Borges's world works so well, in a text that occupies the literal and metaphorical centre of both collections, makes the rest of the book ride easy in the mind.

We needn't go into what precedes and what follows this primary story in any detail. The rest is all pure Hughes: madcap and pedantic, hilarious and depressive, chocabloc and emptied of all but echoes, metropolitan and provincial, glittery and blacker than black. It is time to close this introductory text. It is time to dive into Pandora's Box.

Preface to the Unpublished Edition

I might define as Borgesian that excessive interest in possibilities which never (or rarely) succeeds in exhausting itself with awe, terror or time. It is not a postmodern style in any academic sense. The imposition of the past on the work in progress is natural and clever, not forced and smart. Indeed, any imitation of Borges must be based more on his influences than on his own creations. It is futile to seek, in his technique, clues to the future direction of fiction. The answer is somehow already in the past, made anew by the logarithms of mutable language, rather than by the posthaste arrival of the next horizon. I do not really know what I am suggesting, but with the passage of years it may come to sound intellectual, in which case it will also be baroque, smug with its own tricks and life. Provided the remainder of our lives are happy, this is irrelevant.

The very title of this little book flaunts its Borgesian character. To apologise for it would be tantamount to admitting I am incapable of paying the great man tribute. I prefer to keep admissions of such weakness to myself, however obvious they may be. Borges was perhaps the greatest fiction writer of the previous century. His first book of prose, *Historia Universal de la Infamia*, was published in 1935 and consisted of seven relaxed essays, one short story and eight fake fragments. The following slim volume follows it almost exactly but with a wink. My own pieces are insolent in their desire to ape the originals, which themselves were boldly and charmingly irresponsible. They are the game of a mildly shy but not very young man who dared to write stories but wanted to pretend that he composed other pieces too. Even this Preface, which I did not wish to write, because I could think of nothing sensible to say, was deemed necessary to match my model. In fact, two Prefaces have been included, because that is the number which appears in the edition I own.

It is fun to lie and not be caught. One of the best ways of doing this is to admit the lie beforehand, so there is nothing to catch. As with the originals, my essays are not rigorous. They are fundamentally correct, but rumours have been recorded as facts with minimal disapproval. The most outrageous details are frequently the truest. And if you believe that, you might as well believe anything. Nonetheless it is so. As for the short story, it is puff and blather, and the difference and distance between it and the story it pretends to shadow is larger than any other object and shade in this project. To be honest, there is no shadow at all, merely a blot of darker blackness amid the general gloom and collapsed murk.

The essays are violent and vile, and for that I *do* apologise. Unfortunately, the original Borges book was also violent, and it would have been a betrayal to write a history, universal or specific, of gentleness and timidity. My fragments are short and slight, and falsely attributed to authors other than myself. Some of these authors are real people and at least two are still alive and may not be flattered by the attribution. That is possibly how it should be. The fragments are followed by a section which has no counterpart in the original book. The three parodies contained in this section should therefore be left unread to make the tribute to Borges more authentic. However, one of them is a parody of my own writing style as perceived by the reader. Parodying *myself* in the style of *you* is the hardest parody I have ever attempted, because you are an individual rather than a type and also because I almost certainly have no real idea who you are or how you might write. On this note I leave you. Farewell! Sleep soundly in your bed tonight and have a dream on me.

Preface to an Imaginary Edition

The exercises in narrative prose that make up this book were written in a period of just over ten years. They stem, obviously, from my readings of Borges and have been fortified by an acquired taste for *yerba mate* tea. They exploit certain tricks of the ironic trade and are subject to the lesser infamies which exist before and after every page, including a difficulty with coining titles and indecisive celebrations after the completion of each piece. A similar distension gives shape to the story 'Streetcorner Mouse'. The slang in this tale is not Lunfardo but Wenglish. Not the full jargon, but its forced and faint echo.

As for the instances of literary quackery that comprise the 'Et Al' section, they are not, nor do they try to be, cunning. I have more rights to them than those of translator and reader, but I shall pretend I do not. At the same time, worried that credit might be directed elsewhere, I feel compelled to admit the ruse here. If you do not believe me, I may still be safe. Sometimes I suspect that finishing a book and starting it, whether as reader or author, are the only two definitive moments of its existence. The leap from world to word, from word to world. The rest is cluttered emptiness. Or maybe not.

A NEW UNIVERSAL HISTORY OF INFAMY

The Brutal Buddha
Baron von Ungern-Sternberg

The Blank Page

In the history of Mongolia, the blankest page is the 19th century. After the collapse of the Ming dynasty, the usurping Manchus consigned the country to an obscurity which made its name synonymous with the edge of nowhere: the economy was handed over to unscrupulous traders who used a loophole in the law to blackmail the populace. When a Mongol fell into debt, a merchant would threaten to kill himself. A man who drove another to suicide was charged with murder.

In the grasp of the businessmen, the capital, Urga, enjoyed immense debasement and impenetrable mystique. Two Europeans who managed to visit it during this time were Luigi Barzini and Scipione Borghese, an Italian journalist and count who were racing an automobile from Peking to Paris. This was in 1907, when Urga was still a town of filth and decay. Streets were infested with dogs who attacked any commuter not equipped with that essential part of everyday attire: a stick barbed with iron. Disposal of bodies was a relatively painful affair: dying relatives were simply left out at night for the hungry hounds.

Here we have another clue as to the eccentric legal system favoured in Old Mongolia. A corpse untouched by dogs was deemed extremely unlucky and the surviving family of the deceased was in danger of being arrested for spreading dissent. Urga's prison was rated as the worst in the world and each room of the complex was piled high with wooden crates less than four feet in length. These coffins served as cells – unable to sit up or lie at full length, the hapless and starving prisoners were also weighed down with lead chains and manacles.

When the Mongolian people finally took the chance to revolt against foreign rule, a king was chosen – Boghd Khan, eighth reincarnation of an ancient Buddhist deity. Independence lasted only two years. The Russians and Chinese united to divide the country between them and the Boghd Khan devoted himself to the genus of debauchery that was to leave him a blind syphilitic within the decade. It was at this point, in the early 1920's, that two idealists came to his aid.

The first, Dambijanstan, was a bandit who heaped humiliation on the Chinese by defeating their armies in the western deserts. Stealing sight was the speciality of this ambiguous hero, who employed sheep's knuckles for the purpose: bound at the temples and tightened with a dozen twists, they caused the eyes of his victims to bulge sufficiently for them to be snipped free with a pair of scissors. Dambijanstan was very careful with his trophies, storing them in the lining of his tent until the smell and staining of the silk became unbearable. Then he would catch the culprits of this desecration – the men he had blinded – and punish them by making furniture-covers out of their skin.

Worse than Dambijanstan was the man responsible for ruining the bad name of Mongolia. Ostensibly a freedom fighter and friend of the people, he turned out to be their rival, unwittingly pushing them into the hands of the communist Red Army and ensuring that the nation became the second Marxist state, at complete cost to a millennia-old culture and heritage. For the span of a single year he carved out what can be described as the most anomalous system of government in the modern era. During his reign, this remote realm exchanged dominion by imported tyrants for a nightmare perversely based on Buddhist faith.

THE BARON

Roman Feodorovich von Ungern-Sternberg was an archetypal 'White' Russian extremist. Born in 1886, a Baltic German, he claimed descent from a long line of military men, including Attila the Hun. During the Crusades, his ancestors gained the reputation of being in league with Satan. Certainly they were mentally impeded. Ungern-Sternberg himself was the proud owner of an atrophied brain, a feature he used to demonstrate his relationship with the dwarfish Attila. It was housed in an unnaturally small cranium, described by one follower as being cloven by "a terrible sword cut which pulsed with red veins." An ascetic and lopsided expression combined with broad shoulders, disordered blond hair and lipless mouth made him appear like an excruciating example from the local demon pantheon. Fortunately, no photographs of his visage exist*.

Ungern-Sternberg served with another vicious 'White', the notorious Grigory Semenov. They fought together in the Carpathians and were posted to Siberia at the same time. One of Ungern-Sternberg's favourite hobbies after he was promoted to the rank of Major-General was to enter taverns, consume enough vodka to achieve double vision and then fire at the other patrons, logging how many he could hit. To his astonishment, it remained a constant fifty percent of those he aimed at. Despite his tiny head, it took enormous quantities of alcohol to make him drunk. After a few years of developing his hobby, drinkers across Siberia learned to flee when he kicked open café doors with a boot.

The Baron felt the pull of the East: the mountains, rolling steppes and icy wastes of Genghis Khan's stamping ground. He studied the tactics used by Mongol warlords and was fascinated by their courage and stamina. When his total of dead customers became too high for his addled brain to recall, he was struck with a revelation. He later compared this blast of insight with satori, the enlightenment experienced by Buddha. This noble divulgence was as follows: by slaying people he was doing them a favour. If they were unable to protect themselves, it meant they were feeble and living under poor karma. By dying in a state of innocence, they improved their position on the rungs of the cosmos. It dawned on Ungern-Sternberg that his tawdry victims were destined to be reborn as greater beings. He was thus the agency of their improvement, a holy man destined to aid all those who still clung to such material values as air. In the blink of an ill-set eye, the Baron became a convert to the eightfold path, preaching respect for life with a bullet. In his newfound wisdom, he realised that

* With the rumoured exception of a badly developed image taken by a certain 'Mikhail Simanov' which has been privately circulated but never copied or published."

he must interpret the scriptures in his own manner. For good measure, he dissolved a dose of apocalyptic Christianity into the brew, like a pinch of arsenic in a dish of butter tea.

SEARCH FOR MEANING

Now the Baron had belief, he also had a purpose. The Bolsheviks, already sweeping Marxist-Leninism to every corner of the empire, were a tangible manifestation of Mara, the evil essence. They had to be exterminated: by dying in agony they would be reborn as superior 'White' Russians. Unable to make calculations more complex than those which could be performed on his unnaturally long fingers, the Baron reasoned that for every 'Red' he murdered, his own ranks would swell with two more soldiers. The dead man counted both as one away from the enemy and one for himself. When it was pointed out that the souls were not reborn into maturity, but as babies, he hired soothsayers by the score for elucidation. These also counselled caution; with inherited and borrowed wealth he conscripted them into the nucleus of his private bodyguard.

To take on the Red Army, however, was above even Ungern-Sternberg's delusions. Nor could he stay longer in Russian territory. The answer was simple – he would ride into Mongolia, destroy the Chinese administration and set up a personal kingdom. Then he would forge a Pan-Asiatic empire, including Manchuria and Tibet. As his magical powers increased in tandem with his military strength, a proper invasion of his motherland could be undertaken. At this stage, his scheme included the dismantling of Moscow and its replacement with a city of tents. He saw stone cities as hubs of evil; their solidity made concrete the miseries of existence. An officer under his command remarked on his genuine conviction that he was a force for good in the universe. In the Baron's words: "Only evolution leads to divine truth; I am that process."

The Holy Plan

When Ungern-Sternberg had managed to enlist over three hundred devotees, he baptised them in vodka and hashish and gave them a name: the Order of Military Buddhists. To prove the mind stronger than the flesh, the Baron decided to reverse Buddha's moral guidelines. Narcotics were to be taken at least once a day but celibacy was mandatory. Any true follower of the path shuns the first but is not strictly required to forsake the latter. The reasoning of the Baron was that if he could sin against his religion and yet preserve his faith, he was more than a disciple; he was a saint. The Order of Military Buddhists dazedly entered Mongolia in 1920, partly chased out of Russia by Bolsheviks.

On horseback, they reached Urga in February 1921. Mongolian winters are incredibly severe: temperatures of minus 40° C are not uncommon. Unable to launch his attack without astrological guidance, Ungern-Sternberg set up camp outside the gates, awaiting a beneficial alignment of the stars. Eager to taste the heated delights of the city, his soldiers whiled away the hours by debating the virtues of necrophilia. Finally, at a divinely ordained moment, the Baron released his frostbitten crew of savages upon the capital. They encountered scant resistance as they stampeded through the narrow alleyways and courtyards. Baffled imprecations from merchants formed the biggest counter attack. The carnage was atrocious: an orgy of rape and looting lasted three days.

One of the Baron's officers, Dmitri Alioshin, left a garish account of the assault and its aftermath. The soldiers broke into shops, dragged priceless silks into the dirty alleyways and swathed themselves in grimy finery. The small Jewish population was completely exterminated, in true Russian style. "Drunken horsemen galloped along the streets shooting and killing at their fancy... The humiliation of the women was so awful that I saw one of the officers run inside the house with a razor and offer to let the girl commit suicide before she was attacked..." This was a trick as celibacy applied only to relations with living women. A new method of executing men was invented – they would be forced to stand at one end of a street while a rider armed with a block of wood swept past and smashed them in the face. One Military Buddhist, a Cossack, started shooting his own men in mistake and was retired.

THE AFTERMATH

After cleansing Urga of Chinese influence, Ungern-Sternberg settled down to the business of consolidating his victory. To prove his skills in the field of peace, he restored the Boghd Khan to the throne and disinfected the city sewers. Then he embarked on a sequence of reforms, which helped to turn the picturesque and dangerous capital into the soulless place it has remained since. But positive results came from some of his ideas. He introduced paper currency, built bridges and arranged a public transport system. He founded a library of religious texts and opened schools where Mongols could study their culture.

There have been many autocracies throughout history, but surely few as outlandish, in both senses, as the one inaugurated by our Baron. Most dictatorial crimes spring from egos which have spiralled out of control; Ungern-Sternberg wanted nothing to do with his own ego. A fine Buddhist, his mandate was to free himself and others from the fetters of identity. He was fond of tapping his head, with its duelling scar, and exclaiming: "Even this is too big for my needs." Thus his outrages were conducted in the spirit of violent serenity. Death was the reward for good behaviour; to catch the favourable karma before its owner could negate its effects. Wrong behaviour was also punishable by death, a slower one. Citizens who used his bus service but disembarked at the "rebirth station of the day" were suspended from a tree and gently lowered into an enormous fire. The Baron termed this a "return fare."

It is said that Urga's children in the summer of 1921 were superbly educated. Food was scarce in the city at that time – school dinners were not readily available. At the end of each morning, those dunces still at the back of the class became main course for the more capable. But those at the very front became pudding. It was a question of moderation in all things, including arbitrariness. Secular thieves were believed to suffer from a virus caught from the Chinese. The Baron devised an original form of complimentary medicine to treat such patients. His range of cures was remarkable, from "funnel-consumption" of arkhi, the local brew fermented from mare's milk, to "sewing mice into the liver." Most reliable of all, was the big enema with turpentine.

Whether every tale which surrounds the Baron's excesses is entirely factual is open to debate. Bolsheviks surely played up his monstrousness after his death. One grotesque fabrication worth mentioning is his habit of wriggling inside a horse's stomach to look for "equanimity." He could enter the beast from either end. "With his minuscule head, hardly bigger than a man's fist, it was little trouble for him to climb his way into a snorting steed." He started asking his own men to donate their skeletons for the construction of a "multi-jointed Bodhisattva." Unanimously, they refused. Ungern-Sternberg wept for the lost chance to skip reincarnation and achieve instantaneous Nirvana.

THE KETTLE DEMON

Rumours are lies in fog, but independent witnesses attest to the cruelty of his two favourite minions. The first of these, Colonel Sepailoff, was given the rank of Commander of Urga. Suffering from a form of Tourette's Syndrome, "always nervously jerking his body," he sang wordless songs as he killed people. The second lackey was a man who had forgotten his name in the long ride across the Mongolian steppe. As no-one else recalled it and he was always brewing tea, he received the nickname 'Teapot'. He was the Baron's constant companion. Whenever a Mongol applied for a job with this new administration, Ungern-Sternberg would personally interview the candidate. If he requested a cup of tea during the proceedings, 'Teapot' would move behind the job-seeker and strangle him with his steamy hands. Expiry did not necessarily disqualify the candidate from being offered a position, nor from earning a wage.

THE COLLAPSE

Naturally a government run by lunatics and rotting cadavers could hardly hope to be accepted seriously on an international stage. The British had lined the pocket of the Baron's acquaintance, the demented Semenov. When this money ran out, Semenov crumbled. In a similar way, Ungern-Sternberg managed to last eight months merely because of financial assistance from Japan. The details of this assistance are unknown; undoubtedly Tokyo saw an independent Mongolia as a useful bulwark against the Russian bear and Chinese dragon. Power politics in the area at this time remain extremely shady, like a mirror in a dungeon.

The demise of Ungern-Sternberg was precipitated by his treatment of the Boghd Khan. The Baron had embarked on a campaign to improve the soul of Urga. This involved incarcerating each citizen in turn in the prison. The captives were supposed to remain in the crates until someone came to buy them out. This served both to raise revenue and earn "wondrous karma all-round." The person who paid the money gained one share for freeing a soul in torment; the individual in the cell earned another for being the cause of the former's altruism; the Baron also earned a part for setting up the system in the first place. The Boghd Khan asked the Baron if this was pushing liberal religion too far. Ungern-Sternberg patted him on the head and announced that he would take up his objections with Buddha when he visited Heaven. "But first you must lend me your loftiest ladder," he continued, glancing up at a cloud.

This was too much for the king, who issued a request for aid to all who felt strong enough to offer it. A young communist heard the plea and took up the flag of justice. Sukhe Bator was everything Ungern-Sternberg was not: disciplined, courageous without being reckless, possessed of an ordinary head. A former dispatch rider, he was the founder member of the secret People's Party, an opposition group based in the desert. With six representatives, including the insane Choibalsan, Sukhe concealed a copy of the Boghd Khan's request in the handle of a bullwhip and smuggled it to Russia. When he came back, it was at the head of a Red Army division. For Mongolia, it was the start of seventy years of different intolerance and anguish as a Soviet satellite.

The Broken Talisman

Ungern-Sternberg did not wait to welcome defeat in the ruins of Urga. He decided to take the fight to the Bolsheviks. He rounded up his followers and charged north. To prepare for the impending conflict, double rations of vodka and hashish were issued. His drugged army was quickly decimated by a communist patrol. The survivors mutinied and attempted to shoot the Baron. He fled, without hat or clothing, into the night. One description endures from this period: "On his naked chest numerous talismans, charms and medals were hanging on a yellow cord. He looked like a reincarnation of a prehistoric apeman. People were afraid to even look at him." As he sought to evade capture, Sukhe Bator invaded Urga, renaming it in honour of himself – Ulan Bator. One by one, Ungern-Sternberg lost his remaining men. He was the last to be caught.

He was taken to the Siberian city of Novosibirsk by train. At every station he was exhibited on the platform as a freak in a cage. No charge was levied to stare at him. His trial was swift and callous, yet for the first time in his life, he spoke coherently. He remained unrepentant but the mysticism had evaporated. He was the last 'White' general to trouble Lenin; the revolution was settled.

In September 1921 he was sent before a firing squad, still weighted down with talismans. His last utterance was to accuse his judge of being "too red." His head was much too small to make a suitable target, so the marksmen aimed for his chest. Shrapnel from a charm seriously injured at least one of them. His brain was removed for study by doctors and it was disclosed that his left lobe, now considered the hemisphere of identity, existed only as a shrivelled root.

Coda

When the news of his demise reached the Boghd Khan, the king prepared an elaborate memorial service to be held for the benefit of his ghost. Some of the prayers spoken that evening were attempts to ensure the Baron was never reincarnated anywhere in Mongolia. The Boghd Khan led a procession through the city streets in an ox-powered automobile, a present from the Russian ambassador, who had neglected to explain how to start the motor. Devastated Urga had not yet escaped Ungern-Sternberg's malign influence. Further structural damage was caused by the all-night beating of massive silver gongs and improbable drums.

The Honest Liar
Denis Zachaire

The Burned Fingers

The blistered hands of alchemists are worth no more on the open market than those of cooks, firemen or blacksmiths, but they are more likely to remain concealed in pockets in public. In certain ages the profession of *transmuter* was a dangerous one and any scholar who wore scorch marks on his flesh risked the fate of Pietro d'Apone, racked to a long death by the Inquisition of Padua. Although alchemy relied on chemicals rather than devils, some authorities punished it with the penalties recommended for sorcery. John de Rupecissa was starved to a skeleton in a Vatican dungeon for dabbling with the art and the Pontiff was disgruntled to discover that his bones were not made of gold. Possibly more fortunate was Ortholani, who in the winter of 1358 was burned at the stake in a Parisian street with small bags tied around his neck which contained the strange dust he had been caught mixing in his basement. This turned out to be a crude form of gunpowder and killed both him and his executioner almost instantly.

The suspicion that official harassment of alchemists had more to do with frustration at their unprofitability than hatred of magic should here be raised. Even the greatest masters of the discipline continually failed to manufacture gold. Bernard of Treves eventually managed it at Vienna in 1461 with a process involving aquafortis, mercury and dung, but the amount of yellow metal which emerged from his crucible after months of heating was only a third of what he originally put in. Embarrassed by this result, he left Europe and voyaged to the Orient to seek alternative and cheaper methods, which proved no less elusive than at home, for he always made a loss. He died penniless in 1490, having come to the conclusion that the real aim of alchemy is to add value to the gold which already exists by increasing its rarity.

The few adepts who became rich were invariably swindlers. A typical ploy was to borrow money from gullible patrons to buy expensive equipment and then vanish overnight, only to reappear in another city and repeat the trick. One of the boldest was a poor student who adopted the pseudonym 'Artephius' and claimed to be several thousand years old, hoping to raise enough funds by this deception to pay his university fees. Reading as many alchemy textbooks as he could find, he learned that the esteemed Geber had once declared that all metals are really gold but that most of them are sick. Disease alone is responsible for copper, tin, nickel and the rest. Armed with the relevant quotation, Artephius persuaded his clients to wrap iron anvils in blankets and put them to bed, massaging them with scented oils or pressing warm poultices to their surfaces as if they were human patients. He charged large sums for a consultation and hinted that he had personally advised the richest kings of antiquity. His superb memory and confident air never betrayed him, even when he was asked precise questions about the historical personages he cited as close friends.

A similar method was employed by Cagliostro, though he was unmasked when he attempted to sign a cheque in the name of the ancient sage, Apollonius of Tyana. His brief, glorious career began in Palermo in 1760 when he started the rumour that he was a *failed* alchemist and had sold his soul to the devil in exchange for the secret of the philosopher's stone, that mystic egg capable of turning dull bars into shiny ingots. His neighbours found it easier to trust a man who admitted his incompetence at transmutation and flocked to bargain for his stone. He finally accepted the highest bid, sixty ounces of gold, and handed over the painted pebble in question. Then he made haste to leave Palermo. He wandered through many nations until a shipwreck cast him on the shores of Malta, where he was received and befriended by Pinto, the Grand Master of the Knights of St John, a man fascinated by alchemy. Letters of introduction written by Pinto proved useful in securing for Cagliostro a position at the French Court, where he dwelled in luxury until the mistake of the forged signature replaced ease with incarceration.

The Subterranean Flower

Failure at alchemy as a means of making money was a stratagem exploited by one other adept, but he went further than Cagliostro and never spent a single night in prison. In 1527, the University of Bordeaux accepted a new student by the name of Denis Zachaire. As the only son of a noble but impoverished family he was expected to pass exams and obtain gainful employment as rapidly and efficiently as possible. He chose to study law. On his first day, confused by the myriad passages and interlocking chambers of the college buildings, he turned up at the wrong class. By the time he realised his error it was too late. He had graduated as a professional apothecary who specialised in preparing medicines from minerals. Too ashamed to return home, he opened a shop and acquired a reputation as a reliable healer.

His jars were always well stocked with beneficial substances such as arsenic, lead and mercury, but one morning he noted he had run low on sulphur, essential for skin complaints. It was a time of plague and his delivery boy had died. He decided to fetch the sulphur himself, from his usual source, a merchant who dwelled in a house on the edge of town. His face enclosed by a metallic beak stuffed with rose petals to overpower the smell of death, which as everyone knows is the only way disease can spread, he ventured onto the street. Rotting corpses filled the gutters. The merchant's house stood alone in a forest. A dog ran whimpering from the apparition which strode toward the front door and rapped loudly for admittance. There were sounds of activity from within but nobody came to answer. With some trepidation, Denis tried the handle. It turned and the door swung open.

The noises came from the cellar, a heavy wheezing and hissing, as if an asthmatic giant was lurking there. Creeping down the steps, Denis entered a model of hell. Crouched over a huge bellows, the merchant was fanning a furnace on which stood a crucible of noxious liquid. Removing his beak in the heat and dropping it with his perspiring fingers, Denis attracted the attention of the experimenter, who turned to confront the intruder. Extending a white hot poker, the merchant politely requested a solemn vow from the newcomer to become his assistant in the clandestine operation or be unofficially branded a trespasser. Denis was intrigued. He was a believer in the principles of transmutation but had never considered applying them himself. Now he had a golden opportunity, pun justified, to turn theory into practise. He accepted the merchant's offer. At a nod from his new tutor, he stooped to retrieve his beak and cast it into the crucible. Without its protection it was impossible for him to return home. Arcing across the room, it quietly shed its petals.

UNEXPECTED HEADWAY

For three months, master and pupil toiled to convert common metal into gold. Rarely venturing outside the cellar, existing on a few slices of bread and one flask of water a day, sleeping on straw in a corner, they diligently followed the instructions of an alchemical manuscript which the merchant had unearthed in a sealed box in the forest while digging for truffles. Some of the symbols used in certain formulae were obscure and they attributed their repeated failure to a misunderstanding of these unknown shapes. The merchant agreed to send Denis back to the town and the university library, where he might achieve clarification. The plague had now passed. With a promise to return as soon as possible, Denis made his way home. In his absence, his business had collapsed and thieves had taken most of his possessions.

At first he enjoyed his liberty from the stifling atmosphere of the cellar. He wrote to his family for a loan, pretending to need money to attend a lawyer's conference, and received the sum of two hundred crowns. With this he refurnished his home and bought drugs for his shop. His customers began to reappear. But his mind was in turmoil. At last he visited the library and consulted every work of alchemy on the shelves. In a copy of Albertus Magnus's *Coy Wisdom of a Brazen Head*, he learned that some men are destined for alchemy. From this moment he was lost to honest science. Sleep eluded him and he dreamed of labyrinths of gold and infinite sequences of yellow gates opening before him. Finally he was unable to resist the call another day. Leaving his front door open, he walked back to the forest and the merchant's abode. The dog had starved on the lawn and the sounds from within were fainter than before. There was bubbling and hissing but no wheezing. At the bottom of the cellar steps he discovered the crucible cooling over fading embers. His initial thought was that the merchant was taking an absurd bath. As he stepped forward he realised the head was floating free on the surface of the liquid. The body below had dissolved and there was no blood. Desperate or inspired, the merchant had experimented with a new ingredient.

THE WAX PLUG

Pondering his options, Denis concluded he was now the rightful heir of the merchant's quest and property. He cleaned out the crucible and relit the furnace. The manuscript they had been working from was obviously a fake and needed to be reburied in the woods. Denis preferred to put his faith in Raymond Lully, Nicholas Flamel, George Ripley, Cornelius Agrippa, Paracelsus and other 'respectable' alchemists, whose books were available at the library. As his studies progressed he began to wonder whether the real meaning of alchemy had nothing to do with gold but was a secret philosophical or ethical system which used recipes as metaphors. In one of Basil Valentine's volumes he found the following curious process:

> **"Take six parts of the king of regrets, one pinch of shadow, clarified and sublimed; and one part of the mood of the moment. Put ingredients into a starlight-encrusted glass vessel, add vinegar, close up with the lute of wisdom. Simmer a month over seductive winks; pour the whole into a unicorn's horn; seal with sand and immerse in a pool of cyclops' tears while whistling the ninth song of the sirens. Distil, at a furious heat, the contents of the horn, and there results a glutinous fluid, which is none other than the yolk of the cosmic egg."**

The blatant impossibility of such a procedure led him to suspect a coded message, but he was at a loss to determine what it might be about. He conjectured it was a method of improving one's mental health or else optimising a man's behaviour in society, but as these remained baseless speculations he did not devote too much time or energy to proving them. Instead he returned to the idea that alchemy can transform base metals into gold. Still his experiments came to nothing. At last he exhausted every technique in every borrowed book to no avail. He required yet more volumes by different authors and perhaps the company and wisdom of other alchemists. He sold every ornament in the merchant's house and travelled to Paris, arriving there in early January 1539. He rented a garret and proceeded to seek out fresh tutors.

The city at that time was almost overrun with alchemists, many of whom also traded in crucibles and other apparatus in the street markets. Within a month, Denis had joined a loose guild of enthusiasts who met every night in a different tavern. They all swore by radically diverging theories but none could claim even partial success, arguing instead about trivial points of technique. His doubts growing, Denis rarely contributed anything to the debates, preferring to linger in the shadows and watch. It occurred to him that perhaps alchemy was really about turning sensible men into fools. But he pledged to wait another year before rejecting the art. He worked as an apothecary in the daytime and spent his wages on equipment and books. At night his garret window glowed with unhealthy colours.

A rumour began among the guild that an authentic master had arrived in Paris, a man who could create gold from simple domestic substances in hours rather than months. This man refused to give his name, pleading that he was already known by so many he had no wish to increase their number. When challenged to give one of these other names he shrugged and replied, "I was once an Egyptian pharaoh and a general of Alexander the Great and Julius Caesar but more recently I have been resting from fame." He was fluent in every language unknown to anybody else. Denis bought his friendship at a high price. Alone and drunk in the rear room of a filthy tavern, the master offered to manufacture gold that very night in the garret. They lurched back through the narrow streets in the rain, Denis excited to an almost unbearable degree.

The master asked for a crucible and into this he poured wine, salt and dirty water. Then he boiled the mixture over the coals, stirring it with his wand and muttering in a low tone. The liquid seethed and filled the room with steam. Pocketing his wand, the master backed away to a chair and waited for the crucible to boil dry. Denis was shocked by the simplicity of the ingredients and operation. When the liquid had disappeared, he moved toward the crucible and looked within. At the bottom lay a coating of gold dust. He fell to his knees in joy but was helped up with a mocking laugh. The whole process was a trick, a piece of theatre. Any liquid was suitable, provided it was opaque. The master showed Denis his wand, which was hollow and open at one end. Then he explained how it worked. First it was filled with a quantity of gold dust and the end was plugged with wax. As the boiling liquid was stirred the wax melted and the gold dust poured out and sank to the bottom. Evaporation revealed it again.

The master planned to dupe rich patrons with this method. The gold dust was his only expense. After he had convinced observers of the power of his alchemical procedure, he would request funds for more equipment and then suddenly leave Paris. It was an old fraud. He invited Denis to become his partner in crime. But Denis was formulating his own plans. He had decided to become a debunker, a great public cynic, an exposer of chicanery, a revealer of secrets, a traitor to swindlers, the scourge of charlatans, and to make a comfortable living by doing so. The mechanics of deceit would give him wealth *within the law*. It was obvious and brilliant. Honesty about dishonesty for the sake of profit! There was a horrible purity in this course of action, an alchemy of motives and perspective. And the master would be his very first victim.

Carnival of Lies

In 1542 a mania gripped the wealthiest citizens of Paris. A showman who dressed in a mask like a beak and who refused to give his name or reveal details about his life, other than that he was *no older than he seemed*, began giving private performances of a wondrous nature. The fashionable and curious battled with each other to hire his services. He would turn up after sunset accompanied by a dwarf who carried his equipment and in a cool but authoritative voice announce an experiment to open the eyes of the ignorant. After his first presentation, certain arrests were made. This set a pattern for subsequent shows. He soon found himself a hero of the angry noblemen and bankers who coughed his fumes out of their lungs.

Within a short space of time he learned to manipulate an audience with the skill of a great actor. But the demonstration was remarkable enough by itself. As one unnamed source put it, "With rare dexterity the alchemist makes gold again and again by methods which seem genuine, then he reveals the trick by which this happens... Also he explains the foolish techniques of the masters of old and how worthless they are in every way... He puts iron anvils to bed but none get well... He accepts payment only in gold, some of which he uses in his experiments, and keeps a careful record of all his earnings... Repeatedly he insists he has never known any historical personages nor even been one himself..."

Although he never removed his mask, he took few real pains to conceal his identity. He spent most of his free time researching flawed alchemical methods and learning new tricks. He was now the bane of his old friends, who were reduced to worse poverty by the ridicule he cast on their work, and the guild put a price on his head, which they were unable to create in their crucibles. Thus he remained safe. He planned to hone his skills until he was familiar with every known method of every known alchemist. He hired more assistants to help with his show. Soon he had acquired a carnival devoted to the single aim of exploiting the innumerable kinds of alchemical lie. He published his autobiography, *The Masked Unmasker*, and wandered the libraries and bookshops of Europe seeking obscure titles. One morning in Toulouse he chanced on a manuscript no larger than the palm of his hand. It appeared to be the key to a mysterious code. Leaving his show in the hands of his assistants, he rode off somewhere. He returned exactly one month later, happy and smelling of fungi.

THE FINAL IRREGULARITY

Denis Zachaire relocated to Lausanne in Switzerland, where he bought an enormous mansion. He continued to experiment with alchemy but no longer bought books or visited libraries. He stopped putting on shows and announced his retirement, but he continued to lecture on the foolishness of alchemy to any visitors who called. If anything, his insults against the art grew more furious. He gradually became a recluse, rarely leaving his premises. Wheezing and groaning noises only vaguely troubled his distant neighbours, but sometimes he would stand on his balcony and call out wild denunciations of alchemy. After his death, the authorities forced entry into his house and discovered a cache of lumpy gold in his cellar. They also found his accounts in a huge ledger next to his bed. The total sum of gold in the cellar was almost one hundred times as large as the written figure in the book, but they had no way of knowing if this was strange.

CHEWER OF HEARTS
FRANÇOIS L'OLONNAIS

THE SLAVE

Swinging from rigging with a knife between his teeth, the buccaneer of popular legend must take care not to cut his tongue. He will need it later, for some lady whose bodice is already bursting at the sound of his boots on the deck above her cabin. Despite her aristocratic background and refined graces, she will find much to admire in his courage, style and twinkling eyes. He has not changed his shirt for a month, but his embrace will not be sweaty. For this is the buccaneer of swashbuckling fiction, a romantic figure, acrobatic and daring rather than famished and cruel. His breath does not smell of raw flesh and boiled boots. He is a hero-rascal and his teeth are pearls.

The buccaneer of reality is a grosser figure, less inclined to tenderness or elegance. His main motivation is booty and he is willing to acquire it at the extremes of mortal behaviour. This might include dancing with intestines or roasting nuns on a spit. Most terrible of all, the notorious François l'Olonnais leers over the truth of the Spanish Main, plucking out hearts and biting into them, the red juice spurting in his eye before he spits out the beating organ with a blasphemous oath. A slave to danger and fury and revenge, he began his career as a less abstract kind of slave, an indentured servant, shipped out to the island world of the Caribbean while still a boy.

The Framing Device

The buccaneers were not quite pirates, for they acted as semi-legitimate agents of the maritime powers united in common cause against the Empire of Spain. The conquistadores had depopulated the island of Hispaniola by murdering the indigenous peoples. Hogs and cattle took over the forests. From about 1610, desperate refugees from brutal captains and bruising shipwrecks found they could settle there and live by hunting, trading meat with passing vessels for gunpowder and drink. Cutting beef and pork into strips, they smoked it over a fire of bones. This mundane method of preparation gave them their glamorous name. The frame on which the meat rested was called a *boucan* by the Carib Indians.

Their numbers soon swelled with the arrival of religious dissidents from Europe. An independent republic began to emerge in all but name, governed by a strict but rigorously fair system of laws, the Custom of the Coast, a curt and classless code of honour. Disputes were settled by duels. The Spanish attempted to crush their independence and lives, forcing them to relocate to the smaller and more defensible island of Tortuga. But the plan of starving them into history by culling the wild herds on which they depended was a mistake. It compelled the hunters to put to sea in ships and seek an alternative occupation. The result was freebooting and waves of blood.

At first, the buccaneers used canoes, relying on their superior marksmanship. Captured vessels would be added to their own fleets. They fought so well they attracted the attention of those European powers who hated Spain. The governors of the French, English and Dutch colonies in the vicinity started to employ them as privateers, issuing licenses in return for a share of the takings. To patronise a buccaneer became good business. And it became respectable to enlist in their ranks. Servants who toiled on the plantations, many of them transported to the colonies against their will, now had a place to escape to, a society of men who valued freedom, bravery and frantic spending.

The Stiff Art of Playing Dead

François l'Olonnais was one of these labourers. Having developed a vast hatred of the Spanish with his blisters, his first exploits with the buccaneers gave him a chance to display his equally huge courage. He was given command of his own ship and used it to great effect, earning a name for himself identical to that of the devil. He discovered how best to fight the fiercest men: his habit of granting no quarter ensured his victims defended themselves with utmost desperation. As a strategist he was the inferior of many other buccaneers. But his habit of crowding his ship with as many marksmen as possible created its own magic. Hunger and the threat of sinking increased the accuracy of their aim. This simple alchemy turned Spanish flesh into gold.

The pieces of eight flowed back to Tortuga so fast that existing brothels had to be enlarged, and new ones built, so that the coins might all be spent, rather than saved. Then his luck changed. A storm off the coast of Campeche wrecked his vessel. He swam ashore with his men into the arms, raised with swords, of a waiting Spanish patrol. He was wounded, but played dead, while all his followers were massacred. After dark, he rose and limped boldly into Campeche. Here he stole a canoe and sailed back to Tortuga. They were celebrating that week in Havana and the other major Spanish cities, drinking toasts to his death. But already he was plotting his next adventure. Within days of his escape he had obtained another ship and crew.

The Sack of Maracaibo

With the wind in his small sail carrying him to Cuba, l'Olonnais hoped to make a lightning raid on the small coastal town of De los Cayos. He was spotted by some fishermen who rushed to warn the governor of Havana. The governor was a rational man. He did not believe in ghosts. Thus he made only a thin gesture of response, sending a ship mounted with ten cannons to intercept the extinct buccaneer. L'Olonnais waited for this vessel to anchor for the night in an estuary, then he ordered it to be boarded. The Spanish were chased into the hold of the ship, but summoned up again with soft entreaties. Every man who thrust his head through the hatch had it struck off with a rusty cutlass. Mindful of setting a good villainous example to his men, l'Olonnais insisted on discharging this onerous duty himself. More blisters.

As he wrapped his hands in bandages and complained about the girth of certain necks, the cry was raised that another ship had just appeared on the horizon. It was bound for Maracaibo to buy cacao. They attacked instantly. But l'Olonnais was bored with lopping heads: he opened chests with a new blade instead and found it soothing on the fingers. A sailor with a guitar timed his songs to the pulse of the exposed hearts. These were complex tunes, and difficult dances to accompany them, smooth boots on decks slick with gore. When it was done, l'Olonnais stamped below to examine his haul. Many coins glittered in the candlelight. Enough to fit out a fleet for a really big exploit.

Back on Tortuga, he teamed up with another successful marauder, Michel Basque, who was as savage and daring on land as he, l'Olonnais, was at sea. Together they enlisted a force of 666 men and set sail toward the most incredible and feverish realisation of every buccaneer's ultimate yearning. With insatiable appetites and no concept of the future as a place to live, they gave doom two options and blithely accepted both — a city or themselves. As it turned out, doom made its own scrupulously impartial choices.

Maracaibo was too large and well-defended to serve as an obvious target. Thus the soldiers who guarded it were complacent. They played dice in the truncated shade of low houses, keeping close to the walls where the horizon was modest or indolent. It was just after noon when l'Olonnais entered the strait which opened into the harbour. Behind the city, high in the surrounding mountains, tremendously strong and hairy apemen, who perhaps existed only in the imagination of a dozen drunken chroniclers, and the fears of their wives, looked down with primitive wonder at the sails of the invaders. The habit of these monsters, whose skin resisted arrows and lips rejected speech, was to swoop down on bands of passing Spaniards and carry them off for unknown purposes. When l'Olonnais and his fleet entered Maracaibo, they found it empty. They drank to the health of strange apes.

The truth is smoother and straighter. The reputation of l'Olonnais was so terrible that the entire population had fled the previous night. A lone fisherman had brought them the news of his approach, and without waiting for sunrise they abandoned the city. The buccaneers made merry among the pigs, flour and churches. Then they explored the cellars and attics for concealed wealth. They collected all the pieces of eight in every chest, shooting off the locks with pistols and thrusting gnarled hands into the exposed troves. Many coins were cast high. Injuries, some fatal, were caused to foreheads on the descent. L'Olonnais did not care to experiment with gravity in this way. He paced, regretting the lack of free hearts. Finally he could bear it no longer. He called Michel Basque and cut him down while he was still running. There was no moon or stars. No wall displayed the shadow of a crouching figure sawing at ribs with a blade. The possible profile of a human beast bending lower to nip the left ventricle with a black tooth was censored by darkness.

Barber to Buccaneers

Almost everything known about l'Olonnais comes from a single source: the book published by Alexander Exquemelin in 1678. A man with the unusual occupation of trimming the locks and curling the beards of buccaneers, Exquemelin had travelled to the Caribbean and enlisted with the rovers in order to pay his way through medical school. His personal history is relatively obscure. He was born in Harfleur at the mouth of the Seine, but an adolescent experience with a Dutch girl gave him a love for that northern country, which he later decided to adopt as his homeland. He worked for the French West India Company as a secret agent and barber, before defecting to the other side of the law. He sailed with Morgan and took part in the sack of Cartagena in 1697, after his book was written. Suspiciously, his own hair was unkempt.

For two hundred years, it was assumed that he was a pseudonym for a respectable author, Hendrick Barentzoon Smeeks, whose *Krinke Kesmes* is a shipwreck story set in Australia. But Smeeks and Exquemelin were later discovered sharing the same page in the official ledgers of the Dutch

Surgeons' Guild, suggesting they were separate men who merely knew each other. It is likely they collaborated on the infamous journal which has been credited to just one author. A third member of the Guild, Alonso de Buena-Maison, also assisted the venture by translating the manuscript into Spanish for the benefit of those readers who love to learn about their own humiliation. A version done into English became a bestseller. In 1684, Morgan sued the publishers for libel. He won £400 and grumpily celebrated the clearing of his indefensible name with nights and rum.

Exquemelin was a man of varied interests and only mild prejudices. His careful observations on customs, wildlife and cuisine, frequently combined into one episode, are useful and happy. Of his time in Costa Rica, he writes with intelligent innocence. "...When a troop of monkeys has been fired on and one of them is hit, the others immediately gather round and sniff the wound. If there is much blood spurting out, some of them squeeze the wound to check the blood, others get moss from the trees and stick it in the place, while still others fetch certain herbs, which they chew and then press in the wound. I have often observed with great wonder the way these animals stand by each other in time of need and endeavour to help their fellows, though in peril of their lives... These monkeys are tasty and very nourishing..."

It is unclear whether Exquemelin knew l'Olonnais personally. It is said that his chest was scarred as if from a desperate encounter. Some authorities argue that this gash was earned in Cabo Gracias a Dios. A wild tribe of Indians lived there, skilled in the arts of brewing beer from bananas and waging war with arrows. When a warrior died, his wife was expected to bury him with her own hands, leaving food and drink at the side of his grave for fifteen months. Exquemelin frequently helped himself to these offerings after dark. A rumour began that a malignant spirit was visiting the graves. One night he was caught in the act. He was chased down the beach. Perhaps he turned to call something to his pursuers. The arrow grazed his breast. The remainder of his time in the Caribbean was equally hazardous. But he did not die in the forests of Jamaica, the mountains of Cuba or the swamps of Venezuela. He survived and passed his exams.

The Rewards

Rum, Girls, Parrots, Pieces of Eight, Cups, Muskets, Plates, Pipes, Calico, Boots, Lutes, Dice, Maize, Slaves, Hammocks, Brandy, Cakes, Gold, Cards, Knives, Cacao, Silver, Earrings, Chillies, Wine, Silk, Pearls, Horses, Carpets, Rubies, Tobacco, Sugar, Pistols, Slippers, Coffee, Perfumes, Lamps, Cassava, Drums, Mirrors, Hides, Umbrellas, Furs, Ambergris, Gunpowder, Turtles, Curtains, Honey, Papaya, Eggs, Canoes, Emeralds, Plantations, Clocks, Underpants, Dignity, Honour, Respect, Immortality, Fetters, Prison, Gallows.

Allons, Mes Frères, Suivez-Moi

With alligators scrabbling at the sides of his ships, l'Olonnais dabbed his lips and set sail from Maracaibo. During the return voyage he drank only sherry and ate nothing but salt. Once back in Tortuga, he bought a whetstone and a curved sword, thinner and longer than a cutlass. Before the end of the month, he was itching to commence another adventure. His men were enthusiastic. He decided to invade and occupy Nicaragua. First he sailed for Yucatán, mooring off its northern coast and putting ashore alone in a canoe. He instructed his crew to wait for him, however long he was gone. He had heard about mysterious ruins in the interior, stone cities which once belonged to the emperors of a great civilisation but were now the abode of gentle people who wore flowers in their hair. He hacked his way through the creepers.

They came out of the forest to greet him, leading him by the hand and treating him as an honoured guest. Soon he was a god, sitting on the top of a crumbling pyramid and demanding human sacrifice. He cut out the hearts himself with his new blade, filling urns with organs which pulsed in varied rhythms. At dusk he hoisted these vessels on his shoulders and carried them down the steps to his palace. It was as if the echoes of a thousand drums had been trapped in a jar. Some he roasted, boiled, baked or grilled. Many he devoured raw with a light salad. His complexion grew strange, his jowls sagging and the skin of his ears flaking away. A diet mostly confined to throbbing muscle was not entirely favourable to his health. A change was needed. He also required a fresh whetstone. He had worn this one out, sharpening his sword until it became a dagger.

He left the city in flames and rejoined his ship. His men had not betrayed him. They recognised his voice but not his expressions. A storm darkened the southern sky, but he insisted on sailing into it. For days they were punished by waves and bolts of lightning. When the sea calmed, they had no idea where they were. A town stood overlooking a bay. Tired of talking, praying, cursing, they attacked it in gloomy silence. It was on this occasion that l'Olonnais gathered exactly one hundred captives, arranged them in a line and removed the heart from each. But he did not eat them himself. As he progressed along the row, he gave that honour to the next victim. Every doomed man swallowed the heart of his friend one place to the left. This research into symbolic compression was of major interest to the final prisoner, who indirectly digested all hearts prior to his own, and whose own bursting heart was reserved for l'Olonnais.

Again they sailed away, looking for Nicaragua. They approached a group of rocks, the Islas de las Perlas, but misjudged the depth of the sea between them and ran aground on a reef. They managed to get ashore in the canoes, removing the loose contents of the ship in an attempt to lighten it. But it was stuck fast. So they decided to break it up with hatchets and construct a longboat from the timbers. Realising the task would take a long time, they planted the islands with beans and bananas. Six months later, the boat was finished, but it was only large enough to carry half the marooned men. Lots were drawn to choose who was to remain and who to leave. L'Olonnais was exempted from this ritual. He screamed encouragements at his crew as they plunged into the currents of unknown latitudes. The boat was unseaworthy and capsized off the Gulf of Darien.

The Pinch

L'Olonnais swam ashore alone. His followers had drowned. Waiting for him on the sand was a band of Indians. They scratched him with arrows, bound his hands with creepers and made a large fire. Then they hacked him to pieces very slowly, a pinch of flesh at a time, roasting these morsels in front of his eyes. They danced and sang. Before starting on his head, several of the bravest warriors trimmed his locks and curled his beard. They did not reveal where they had learned these modern styles. The tide came in and extinguished the flames. All that remained of the buccaneer was an unusual colouring in the foam of the waves.

TRADER OF DOOM
BASIL ZAHAROFF

MEN OF MEANS

It was said that the economic philosopher and apostle of free trade, Richard Cobden, always began his lectures with one question. Who was the richest man who ever lived? It is not known if he had his own favourite among the handful of candidates. Certainly the same dozen names were cited again and again as answers to his query, and since Cobden's day another dozen have been added.

Some of the most colourful include King Croesus, last ruler of the empire of Lydia, who was so rich that in 550 BC he invented coinage to enable him to spend his surplus money. This is the first known instance of pocket change. But he also owned all the shops and everything that he spent went back to him. He actually made a profit. His name has since become synonymous with wealth.

Other oriental examples may be mentioned briefly. The Majapahit priests of Borneo were so rich that the heaven they believed in was a place of grinding poverty and menial tasks. The inhabitants of the remote kingdom of Guge in Western Tibet were easily able to bribe away any explorers or mapmakers who ventured onto their land, a custom which continued to preserve their secrecy long after the missionary Antonio de Andrede accidentally stormed the capital Tsaparang in 1624 and turned the territory into an independent Jesuit republic. A century and a half later in China, the Widow Ching could afford to buy her way into expertly researched histories of infamy as a 'lady pirate' despite her mild manners and timid nature.

Westerners were no less cunning or lucky at making money. Sometimes they were oblivious of the fiscal power they held. Reinhold Rau, keeper of the last quagga in captivity (and thus the last alive), was unaware that among the Bop tribe the animal was used as currency, each quagga's worth being determined as a percentage of the total number in existence. Consequently, before the beast in his care died at Amsterdam Zoo on 12th August 1883, he owned all the money in the world. A different sort of ignorance afflicted tycoon Jim Brady who bathed in diamonds instead of water and died of infected cuts. Precious metal rather than gems was the weakness of the Vicar of Splott, Lionel Fanthorpe, who possibly stumbled on the only genuine alchemical system coded in a manuscript buried in a French forest. He always denied his wealth but was interred in a solid gold coffin after crashing his solid gold motorbike on its trial run. In life his fingers smelled of truffles.

These characters are all interesting and the stories behind them might be worth telling more fully*. But none provides the real answer to Cobden's slightly insolent question. The man who was richer than anyone before or since was the meanest man of means. He sold armaments. If some of the exaggerated tales told about him are true, he was rich enough to buy all the shops of Lydia, the island of Borneo, the kingdom of Guge, every historian of iniquity, the last quagga and the whole Bop tribe, every diamond in existence, every flake of gold and even every truffle, all on the same morning and at grossly inflated prices. A rumour claims it is dangerous to write too much about him. Seventy years after his death, hired agents supposedly still wander the earth punishing those who gossip unflatteringly about his reputation. He set up a trust fund big enough to pay for ongoing generations of such thugs, who nonetheless abide by strict rules of ruffian ethics. This rumour has absolutely no foundation in fact.

* William Walker who in 1857 "sold Nicaragua down the river and refused a refund when it went wrong" must be excluded from this list. He was rich only in extended metaphors.

THE TAILOR'S SHOP

Basileios Zacharias, who was to become known to terrified governments as Basil Zaharoff, was born in the sleepy town of Mugla in Turkey in 1849. His parents were very poor but they had relatives all over the world. They were ethnic Greeks who had Russified the family name after years spent in exile in the cold Urals. The hillside Ottoman neighbourhoods of Mugla are some of the finest in Turkey. The white houses and the narrow lanes between them, the ornate doors and roofs, the bazaar with its rows of blacksmiths, the leafy boulevards of the new town, are all delightful to travellers but nightmarish to an oppressed minority. Basil was raised among the bloody tensions of his age. When he turned fifteen he was sent to Istanbul to work for his uncle in the cloth trade. Here he also found a position as a volunteer fireman.

The firemen of the twilight era of the Ottoman Empire were distinct from those in most other places at most other times. Little more than gangsters, they started fires rather than extinguished them. The idea of this was that the worried inhabitants of a particular quarter of a city would pay an annual fee to preserve their homes. It was a form of tax, a simple protection racket. Basil prospered at this trade. Feasibly he would have risen to a position of local influence before being stabbed by rivals one dark night down a darker alley. The life expectancy of a fireman was no more than a few years. But on his seventeenth birthday his uncle dispatched him to England. He enrolled in school and in 1870 was given a job as the overseas representative for his family's cloth business. He learned the strategies of board meetings and the etiquette of conferences. In 1872 his uncle sued him for embezzlement and he fled under a pseudonym to Greece.

THE TRAVELLER

Basil settled in Athens and entertained himself by becoming a ferocious reader of newspapers. One day in a quiet café he was approached by a man who requested a light for his cigar. They began talking and discovered a shared interest in politics and world affairs. Basil confessed he needed a job and the man offered to give him one. He was Stefanos Skoulodis, a powerful financier and diplomat. His friend, the gun designer Thorsten Nordenfelt, was looking for an agent to represent his interests in the Balkan countries. Stefanos offered to introduce Basil to Thorsten. That night Basil began writing the diary he would keep until the penultimate day of his life. The substance of this first entry can only be guessed at. The following week he was interviewed by Thorsten and offered the position. He accepted immediately.

During his extensive travels for his new employer, Basil learned to appreciate many languages, customs, cuisines. He enjoyed love affairs, preferring women with red hair. Much later, when he was able to afford to indulge any whim, he would enter restaurants and purchase them on the spot, ordering all women without red hair to leave the premises at once, but in his early career he was gentlemanly enough never to cause offence or create scandal. Not once was he challenged to a duel over the honour of a lady. He practised with the sword and pistol nonetheless and became a reasonable fencer and marksman. He rarely abided more than a month in one place and eventually became familiar with large tracts of Bulgaria, Serbia, Macedonia, Croatia, Montenegro, Slovenia and Greece, the nations within his sphere of operations.

Two adventures from this period of his life stand out. The first is concerned with the time he was waylaid by bandits on the mountain road between Kotor and Cetinje. Before his assaulters had a chance to demand money from him, he offered to buy the rifles which they had aimed at his head. Pleased with his wit, they agreed. When he reached his destination he sold these at the local market. The second took place in Petrich, the murder capital of Bulgaria, home to so many hired killers that the price of assassinations dropped to $7 each. Wandering the streets in search of a hotel, Basil was insulted by a drunken man who stumbled out of a bar and took an incomprehensible dislike to his beard. Ignoring him, Basil continued on his way, but that same night three men burst through the window of his hotel room and threatened him with pistols. The drunk had casually hired them to kill the stranger with the annoying facial hair. Coolly Basil pointed out that seven dollars shared between three would not amount to much and he offered to pay each man a hundred times that amount to kill each other before they completed the contract on him. The room echoed with shots. The next morning Basil came across the drunk and bought him an early drink as a gesture of menace, goodwill or audacity. By the time he returned to his hotel, the maid had mopped up the thick blood, removed the ugly bodies and covered the bullet holes in the walls with cheap paintings.

A Pithy Maxim

In 1888 the inventor Hiram Maxim, creator of the first reliable machine gun, joined Nordenfelt in business and helped to expand the company's interests into Russia. It was now that Basil saw an opportunity to make serious money. He sold arms to the separatists of the furthest reaches of the Russian Empire and then approached the government to offer more sophisticated weapons to quell these rebels. Minor wars raged along the margins of the Czar's domains. Selling arms to both sides simultaneously was a technique he perfected and which was copied by his rivals, usually with less success. He took a keen interest in the engineering principles and mechanics involved in the design and development of new weapons. It was claimed, probably unfairly, that he personally tested prototype guns on condemned political prisoners.

In Moscow, when not attending theatres or the ballet, Basil learned the Russian diplomat's art of manipulative innocence. He became expert at offering bribes without offending a man's sense of honour. To win lucrative contracts he befriended generals and admirals, visiting their homes and pretending to admire some inferior aspect of their furnishings, which he would offer to buy at a vast sum. For instance, he might notice that a chandelier in a spare room was a poor quality glass copy of a crystal original. He would cry with delight, jump on a chair to examine it more closely, announce that he was a collector of antique chandeliers and that this was one of the finest examples he had beheld. With fluttering eyelashes and blushing cheeks, he would shyly inquire if he might purchase it for half a million dollars. The offer was generally accepted. The Maxim Nordenfelt company made incredible profits and Basil became one of its biggest shareholders.

In 1895 the British firm Vickers bought out Maxim-Nordenfelt and Basil's field of operations became even larger. He now moved into Turkey and the Middle East. He took a warped pleasure in revisiting the land of his birth as a man of power, but he never went back to Mugla. Even for a callous villain, the memories were too painful. One cool day, sitting in a lonely café in the high apple-tinged town of Elmali, he was approached by a dusty horseman who rode in from the east. This man was not a Turk. He dismounted and joined Basil for a glass of sweet tea. It was another of those lucky encounters which seemed to pepper Basil's whole life. The stranger introduced himself as Luis Borghese. He was riding from Peking to Paris to judge the condition of the roads in case long distance automobile racing was invented: it was unnatural but not impossible. Basil agreed that self-propelling wheeled vehicles should race each other between those cities. He was honest about himself, admitting that he was an unscrupulous arms dealer interested in the evolution of technology. Rubbing his grimy chin, Borghese related a tale. His young son had a friend whose grandfather claimed to have witnessed an undersea machine somewhere in the Americas. He described this machine in detail. Finishing his tea, Borghese remounted and continued his journey. Basil pondered. On a napkin he drew a diagram of the machine. Then he reversed the napkin and on the clean side sketched an advanced version. Now he had the plans for a workable submarine.

BUBBLES OF CONFLICT

The Turkish government placed an order for five submarines and paid in advance. Reports of giant metallic eels in the Black Sea were dismissed by newspapers as the delusions of drunken fishermen. Within six months, the Greek government also ordered five submarines. Basil was sighted in Athens again. In 1897 the two nations went to war. On land the Turkish troops won easily. At sea matters were less straightforward. A horrible turbulence in the Bosphorus channel was observed by neutral ships in the last months of that year. This deep storm continued for many days and when it finished the surface of the sea was littered with scraps of fabric and broken chairs and polluted with oil. Meanwhile a man with a pointed beard was socialising in London and denying the feasibility of ships which could operate beneath the waves. In his pocket was a copy of the first photograph taken through a periscope, printed by Vickers and privately circulated to its top agents. It showed Istanbul harbour.

A Few Other Crimes

(a) The Boer War.
(b) Deserting his wife at Charing Cross railway station.
(c) Practising black magic with Aleister Crowley.
(d) Burning down a fire station.
(e) The Russo-Japanese War.
(f) The First Balkan War.
(g) Preferring amontillado to sherry.
(h) The Second Balkan War.
(i) Forging documents to become a French citizen.
(j) Developing poison gas.
(k) Colluding in the Armenian massacres.

The Heinous Hero

In France, Basil worked as a secret agent and spy against the invading Germans. It is said that he saved many lives by providing warnings about enemy tactics. He predicted that the Germans would use poison gas in the trenches and encouraged the British to employ a type of armoured vehicle developed from the recently invented automobile which was provisionally known as a *land ironclad* but was soon rechristened "tank". For his brave services, the French government made him a Grand Officer of the Legion of Honour and the British gave him a Knight Grand Cross of the Order of the Bath. He was now so rich that he had no idea what he owned. To avoid the humiliation of buying something that was already his, he commenced a relatively restrained lifestyle. His main indulgence was the purchase of the famous casino in Monte Carlo. He controlled it but never gambled. He spent most of his spare time conducting a passionate and illicit affair with the Duchess de Villafranca, whose mad husband, Francisco de Borbón, assumed that Basil was one of his servants.

As he grew older, Basil decided to make his mark in the arts. He wrote a play entitled *Realms of the Lost* and hired the painter Nicholas Roerich to design the backdrop and sets. The two men quickly fell out. The play itself was a failure, but its plot has led some modern critics to suggest it anticipates the techniques of Samuel Beckett and Herbert Quain. In ten acts, *Realms of the Lost* shows how all objects which can no longer be found have actually slipped into another dimension, a world which contains nothing but these objects. So all the lost men and women must dwell among the lost furniture of our dimension, telling the time with lost watches and eating crumbs of lost food. However, when objects in *that* dimension become lost they end up in yet another dimension which contains even fewer things, and this process continues until the tenth act (and tenth dimension) is reached. Everything there has been lost ten times and in fact very few objects have made it that far. Indeed, that dimension contains nothing but a bare landscape, a road, a tree and two men with the appearance of tramps.

Black Swans and Darker Threats

Under his villa in the foothills of the French Alps, Basil ordered the excavation of a subterranean lake. Here he sailed pedalos, boats powered by pedals, shaped like giant black swans. The webbed feet pushed him and his guests around in circles, lanterns hanging from the rock ceiling, a musician serenading them from the artificial shore. Basil expired here on 26th November 1936, though his body was secretly taken to Monte Carlo for the death to be registered there, in accordance with his wishes. He had already burned the diary he had kept for so many years. In the decades which followed, bank accounts under false names kept being found which contained vast sums of Basil's money. This process continues today. It is said that his followers will not permit anyone to write an article about him which is longer than three thousand words. There is no need to waste even one more sentence on repeating that this rumour has no basis in truth.

The Worm Supreme
Francisco Solano Lopez

Digesting the Past

The guabirá fruit of Paraguay is renowned for inducing forgetfulness. It is a jungle nepenthe. And forgetfulness is a vital tool, equal to blades and dungeons, for honing and seasoning tyrants. One man who acted like a worm embedded in one of these fruits, eternally devouring the past, his conscience and most of his people, was the gross and ludicrous Francisco Solano Lopez, grandson of El Supremo, husband of an Irish whore, useless 'Napoleon of the South', who instigated the most costly war, in terms of relative loss of human life, in history.

Even without embellishments, his career is baroque. The shape made by a man as he wanders the earth, the figure of his existence in space and time, the moral geometry of this tangle and its unravelling: these are impossible or implausible images. Applied to Lopez, perhaps not. A sick flourish in the universe, a rotten bulge on the health of history, yet one fateful enough to crush several thousand tons of humans, like a gargantuan and poorly executed opera ceiling rife with plaster cherubs suddenly collapsing onto a packed audience. Thus was he. Bloated.

The Unexpected Power

Remote and landlocked, poor and strange, Paraguay is certainly among the most obscure states on the terraqueous globe. Panting in a tropical funk between Brazil, Bolivia and Argentina, it is dwarfed by its neighbours, yet remains large enough to conceal mysteries and confound explorers.

A federation of ferocious Guaraní Indians dwelled there before the first conquistadores, under Don Alejio Garcia, arrived in their rusty armour and malarial sweats. The prime instinct of the newcomers was to do what had been done in Mexico and Peru. Blood was anticipated, and dwindling screams and very clever cruelties.

But here the conflict was not so clear. Before swords could become a substitute for tongues, the Indians proposed a sensual truce, inviting the Spaniards and Portuguese to share their homes and women. The forest maidens defeated the sense of racial superiority of the conquistadores. Within a few generations, there were no true Europeans left, merely the descendants of mixed marriages, as tanned and sturdy as wooden huts, but with light eyes. Paraguay was never genuinely absorbed into an external empire. It mostly escaped. The slow pace of life, the humidity and awful horizons, continued much as before.

Spain still pretended to govern it from afar. But the revolution, when it came, found little to struggle against. The first president of an officially independent Paraguay, El Supremo, thought it best to build up his armed forces. He advertised for generals and cannons from France, Italy and Hungary. He paid for them by increasing exports of *yerba mate*, his nation's main crop. This mild narcotic with the taste of a hastily extinguished fire was welcomed by gauchos and ranchers as a balance in an otherwise wholly carnivorous diet. It is addictive and medicinal. By the year of his death, Paraguay was the most formidable and inhospitable military power in South America.

SON OF THE SON

In 1845, a Hungarian aristocrat by the name of Heinrich von Morgenstern de Wisner travelled to Paraguay to seek his fortune in the court of its second president, Carlos Antonio Lopez. The city of Asunción steamed in its own hot mists. Dripping houses and muddy streets which led to paths which led to swamps, some inside the metropolis, greeted his scandalous eye. He had been exiled from Hungary for an unspecified crime. Here he hoped to rebuild his ego. The key to the boorish heart of the dictator was unstinting flattery. Morgenstern became an expert and was promoted to the rank of Lord High Chancellor.

Now he came up against a difficult problem. Carlos died of a fever and was succeeded by his mad son, Francisco. To make his instant mark on local history, the new president began replacing all the old officials. Most were imprisoned. Morgenstern realised that the key to the boorish heart of *this* dictator was unstinting flattery, but directed elsewhere. Francisco cared little for praise. His massive stomach and rotting teeth were constant reminders that sycophants were liars. But his wife had an ear for a kind and extreme word. Morgenstern danced attendance on Eliza Lynch, *La Concubina Irlandesa*, and so preserved his life, his health and his position, in that particular order.

It must not be doubted that Francisco Solano Lopez loved his exotic bride. And she loved his manly coffers. They had met in Paris in 1853. A prostitute from the age of fifteen, Eliza was born in County Cork, moved to Algeria as the wife of an army vet, then ran off into the desert with a Russian cavalry officer. Eventually she found her way to France and an apartment on the Boulevard Saint Germain, where she advertised her skill as an 'instructress in languages'. Rarely have lessons in sundry tongues been conducted with so little talking and so much grunting. But a desire for more than the status of a courtesan would not leave her in peace. At last her monstrous chance arrived.

Carlos had sent his son to Europe in the hope he might be inspired by modern fashions and culture. The scheme was partially successful. The legacy of Napoleon greatly appealed to Francisco. The laws, construction projects, hats and genocide. He wished to adopt these as his own, carry them back to his homeland, match the feats of the diminutive Emperor in war and control. While strolling down the street, Francisco noticed the sign on Eliza's door. He entered, hoping to learn a few words of French. Within twenty-four hours, he had proposed to her. She accepted. The tour was completed as a couple. Queen Victoria refused to meet them. Empress Eugénie was so charmed by her guests that she vomited when they kissed her hand. Francisco was delighted.

A CHARACTER SKETCH

"Sadism, an inverted patriotism, colossal ignorance of the outside world, a megalomania pushed almost to insanity, a total disregard of human life or human dignity, an abject cowardice that in any other country in the world but Paraguay would have rendered him ridiculous, joined to no little power of will or capacity were the ingredients of his character... [He had that] gross animal look that was repulsive when his face was in repose. His forehead was narrow and his head small, with the rear organs largely developed. His teeth were very much decayed, and so many of the front ones were gone as to render his articulation somewhat difficult and indistinct."

Cunninghame Graham,
Portrait of a Dictator, London, 1933

GOING HOME TO HELL

Francisco Solano Lopez and Eliza Lynch finished their jaunt by visiting the Crimea to watch the opposing armies slaughter each other. Then they sailed back to Paraguay. Morgenstern was waiting for them. Together they plotted the glorious conquest of the continent. The workers of Asunción were mobilised to produce uniforms and artillery pieces. The primitive factories violated safety regulations without stopping. Men were called up. Acceptable ages for the army were generous, encompassing every male, fit or not, between the ages of 10 and 70. Morgenstern was permitted to design his own uniform. He eventually decided upon a doublet embroidered with silk frogs and an Astrakhan collar. Lopez and his wife preferred to dress as Napoleon and Napoleonette.

To train his newly expanded forces, Lopez embarked upon a gigantic building program designed to turn Asunción into the Paris of the South. An Irish architect, John Moynihan, was commissioned to create sculptures larger than any in the history of art. He failed to satisfy. Like every person upon whom the presidential disfavour fell, Moynihan was entombed in a cell under the Grand Palace. Here he was tortured for several weeks by a method known as the *Cepo Uruguyano*. It involved utilising the pains of alternate numbness and sensation. The prisoner would be bound tightly in a complex lattice of ropes and knots, the precise order of which has mercifully been lost. To quote Moynihan: "The feet went to sleep, then a tingling commenced in the toes, gradually extending to the knees... the same in the hands and arms until the agony became unbearable. My tongue swelled up dreadfully and I thought my jaw would have been displaced. I lost feeling in one side of my face... I would certainly have confessed, if I had anything to confess..."

When war started, and the troops were all dispatched to die in the jungles, the construction work continued with children too young to bear arms. Slaves between six and ten years old laboured to carry stones from a quarry thirty miles distant into the centre of the capital. Thousands expired of exhaustion while building the National Theatre, the National Library and the ballrooms of Eliza Lynch. The American ambassador at the time, Charles Ames Washburn, a gold-prospector and lawyer, noted that no rest periods were granted to these puny artisans. But for the children of Lopez, extravagance and indulgence was the standard. When Eliza gave birth to her first son, the dictator ordered a 101-gun salute fired off the roof of the Palace. Eleven buildings were destroyed in the city by the vibrations, and one of the cannons backfired, killing fifty men. But Lopez did not allow disappointment to sour his day. In the forest beyond the suburbs, peasants thought a revolution had started. They celebrated with *yerba mate* and guabirá fruit. The next morning, they had forgotten the joy of this reasonable mistake.

The Triple Alliance

Brazilian meddling in Uruguay provided the pretext Lopez needed for war. Paraguay had the largest army in South America, but the three wealthiest countries on the continent were Brazil, Argentina and Uruguay. Declaring war on all of them, Lopez forgot that gold can buy arms. Within a month, his enemies matched his own forces. After a year, they outgunned him ten to one. The capture of Asunción should have been rapid and casual, but for some reason the Paraguayans fought with fanatical bravery. Terror of Lopez was one factor. At the battle of Estero Ballaco, the Paraguayans marched toward their adversaries backward, so they might keep an eye on their president, who kept rows of loaded cannons ready to slay cowards and traitors from behind.

From the outset, the Paraguayans were deficient in provisions. The expensive carpets from the ballrooms of Eliza Lynch were cut up to make ponchos for new recruits. But with virtually no food, these troops often fainted before they reached the front line. The invaders simply ran them through with lances where they found them. In Asunción the civic follies continued to be erected, until the child labourers were also forced into the army. Lopez retired from active service, preferring to throw parties in honour of his wife. Fancy dress balls were held every night. Perhaps understanding the war was already lost, the president proceeded to drink dry the extensive cellars of the Grand Palace. Brandy was his favourite drink. It dulled the pain of his putrid gums and gave him the insight to invent ever more bizarre tactics.

He toyed with the idea of surrounding the metropolis with bales of *yerba mate* and setting it alight, so that the fumes would stimulate the senses of the defenders, steady their nerves, increase the accuracy of their aim. At the same time, millions of guabirá fruits would be pulped and the juice used to adulterate the rivers. The foreign soldiers might drink, forget their objective and drift home. With the encouragement of Morgenstern, Lopez rounded up the bishops of Paraguay and compelled them to declare him a saint, turning any act of political assassination into a damnable heresy. He prayed to himself for a miracle. By 1870, his men had run so short of munitions that the volumes of the National Library were torn page from page and used for squib cases. But his parties never ceased, nor the meaningless pomp: the speeches, ceremonies, creation of ranks and medals for him alone.

Lacking iron and forges to manufacture cannons, the Paraguayans cut down *quebracho* trees and hollowed them out. These wooden guns were much wider and longer than the typical artillery pieces of the day. They spat out projectiles so far they were only effective when the target was too distant to be aimed at properly. All the same, they killed many troops,

Paraguayans included, for they could only be fired three or four times before exploding and shredding the cannoneers with splinters. Pregnant, old or sick women were given the task of lighting these behemoths. There were simply too few men left. Yet somehow the Triple Alliance was unable to secure outright victory. At last it reached the eastern outskirts of Asunción. As soon as he saw foreign banners waving in his streets, Lopez fled into the western jungle in a reinforced coach.

MONSTER IN OILS

He left behind most of his generals and his portrait. A local artist had started work on the picture a year before, taking time off from battles to paint. Posing as Napoleon, the president's belly and bicorne hat were both too wide for the gilt frame. The artist had compensated for this by locating the excess parts, a wave of flesh, the petal of a cockade, on a second picture. This anticipation of the school of surrealism was simply the result of accident and panic, often the best parents for an original style. But Lopez had demanded an authentic likeness. The warts and stubs of teeth dominated the face. His diverging eyes made it appear he could watch every part of a room at once. In the reflection of his drawn sword the artist had wryly depicted himself.

When the invaders finally broke into the Grand Palace, they found this portrait propped on a throne. Lopez had ordered that it should be treated as his real self, bowed down before, served with wine and meals, talked to with reverence. The hooves of the enemy horses and the lances of their riders demonstrated a special appreciation of this work of art. The surviving generals of the Paraguayan army were made to watch. Ritual humiliation was usually followed by execution. In the wars which ravaged South America in the 19th Century, mercy was rarely shown to prisoners. The Brazilians wanted to impale them; the Argentines voted to slit their throats and force them to run a race; the Uruguayans opted for burning. While the ruined portrait was held high, the decision was announced. It has been forgotten, but those who were destined for the cruel death were already applauding with relief.

THE LOST GOLD

The Triple Alliance was split on questions of method but not of purpose, which was the end of Paraguay as a political and military force. In this ambitious aim they failed. The country, albeit with its borders reduced, endured to fight other battles, in particular the Chaco War with Bolivia half a century later. But its recovery was not inevitable. Lopez managed to sacrifice an estimated 95% of his male population. His own grotesque body contributed to that statistic. After leaving Asunción, he relocated to the fortress of Las Lomas Valentinas, in the mountains, which Eliza had already furnished with a piano. She played the pieces of Lizst, whom she claimed to have known personally, tolerably well. Her recitals were interrupted by the sound of the army's *turututus*, trumpets which helped the Paraguayans to keep up their spirits. She ordered them stopped. And soon Las Lomas Valentinas also fell.

This time the president and his wife fled north into the swamps. He took every fighting man still in one piece, the national archives loaded on 600 carts, the piano, and all the gold from the treasury. One by one he had his soldiers shot on suspicion of treachery. He locked his mother and sister in wooden cages and had them trundled behind the other heavy baggage. The piano was abandoned just before they reached Cerro Corá on the limits of their empire. A few days later, the gold was also dumped, for retrieval after the war, in an unknown river. Fourteen witnesses to the hiding place were executed. This hoard, *los tresorios escondidos del mariscal Lopez y su Concubina*, still awaits those who can slip past the spectres of the fourteen, assigned as supernatural guards. That is the legend. The idea was Eliza's. The president was not a superstitious man. The Brazilian cavalry were catching up rapidly and he decided to make a last stand with his stubborn troops.

Thus it was that 409 old men, women and children prepared to meet the onslaught of several thousand mounted soldiers. Lopez busied himself with designing a special medal to commemorate his impending victory. It was a yard in diameter and hammered from gold plate. He wore it on his chest and was unable to stand under the extra weight. He issued further commands from a chair planted in the swamp. Time was running short.

He executed a few more officers and signed his mother's death warrant, blaming her for giving birth to him and thus generating his predicament. Then the enemy charged. He was toppled from his chair by a lance thrust, but crawled his way to an island of reeds. A rifle volley shredded his gasping form.

Eliza Lynch was spared and buried him with her own hands in the mud of a riverbank. A cavalry officer took an interest in her and carried her back to Rio de Janeiro. She lived with him for a year before running away with another man to Venezuela. She eventually moved to London and then back to Paris, returning to her former occupation of prostitute. She saved hard to buy another piano. In a squalid rooming house for destitute ladies in the Boulevard Pereire, she died. The secret of the location of the treasure of a nation dissolved with her into putrescence and obscure rumour.

The Unlikely Consequence

The decimation of the male population of Paraguay was so thorough that the government which replaced Francisco Solano Lopez made polygamy not only legal but compulsory. The few living boys and even fewer men were encouraged to take as many as ten wives. One of the lucky survivors was Morgenstern. The Brazilians found him cowering at the top of a tree. For reasons which can hardly be guessed at, they captured him alive and set him free. Dazed, he limped back to Asunción. He was offered a job in the new government as Immigration Minister. His sole duty was to encourage foreigners to repopulate the country.

He took this responsibility seriously. His efforts bore the best fruit, a fruit no less magical or damaging than the guabirá, in Germany. In 1886, dejected by the rise of Jewish capitalism, fourteen families from Bavaria arrived to found a city, Neuva Germania, in the jungle. They were led by Elisabeth Nietzsche and Bernhard Förster. Against all the traditions of Paraguay, these colonists refused to interbreed with the locals. Their descendants are still there, feeble and inbred to the point of imbecility, mocked by the land, the fevers and perhaps the ghosts.

The Worst Hero
Dick Turpin

Gentlemen of the Road

During the Middle Ages, the only road maintenance carried out in England was by monks. Pilgrim routes were cleared for the benefit of devout travellers. When Henry VIII closed the monasteries, this work ceased. By the end of the Sixteenth Century, there were no easy roads in the entire country. Rutted mud tracks and overgrown paths made journeys by coach a hazardous and slow business. They also provided opportunities for bold robbers on fast horses. The highwayman was born. The first on record was Gamaliel Ratsey, son of a lord, and former soldier in the Irish campaign of the Earl of Sussex. He roamed East Anglia with a sack on his head and slits for his pitiless eyes. Later he constructed a mask in the shape of a hobgoblin with enormous ears which tended to catch on branches. He was knocked to the dirty ground in more than one forest chase. But he eluded justice for several decades, until, typically, the treachery of a friend delivered him to the clumsy hangman.

Another early highwayman was John Clavel, who altered his disguise for each attack. His favourite spot for an ambush was Gad's Hill on the London to Dover road. He bribed the landlords of local taverns and inns to shelter and protect him. His skill at impersonating judges, bishops, nobles, ambassadors and politicians was deemed remarkable. His luck ran out when he accidentally dressed as himself and tried to rob a carriage near Rochester. The passenger was a distant relative who recognised his true face and reported the incident to Clavel's stern father. An arrest followed. But the hangman was cheated of a victim on this occasion, for the court accepted an appeal for mercy. The prisoner was granted a Royal

Pardon on condition that he write a treatise advising passengers how to avoid being robbed on the road. He was also required to serve a year in the army against France. His book sold well and he retired in luxury in 1642, dying just a few months later.

The third pioneer of this profession was Thomas Sympson, one of the few who survived to a ripe age before his capture. He often wore a skirt and preferred to be addressed as 'Old Mobb'. He rode sidesaddle whenever possible and enjoyed a reputation as a gentle spirit. He rarely murdered his victims, never tortured them and frequently blew them kisses. He was even willing to accept cheques. He once robbed Sir Bart Shower in Devon and requested a money order for £150. Binding his victim and storing him under a hedge, he rode into Exeter and cashed the note at a goldsmith's. Then he returned to free Sir Shower. Although he ended his career at the end of a rope, still garbed as a woman, his total number of hold-ups was higher than all his competitors save one. It was noted with astonishment at the execution that the official hangman seemed to be wearing lipstick on his collar. Sympson had buried the majority of his loot. Potentially, he died very rich. He never married.

OTHER NAMES

Thereafter, every disinherited son and gambling debtor wanted to try his luck on the road. There were lady highwaymen too, *highwaymanesses*, angry and vulgar, smoking tobacco and learning to cheat at cards and duel with double barrelled pistols and sabres. Mary Frith was one; Maud Merton was another. Mary knew how to spit across a wide room. Maud could puff eight pipes in one mouth. Very different from this pair was Catherine Ferrers, wife of a lord, rich enough not to rob travellers, but much too bored to resist the adventure. She used a secret passage to move from her bedroom to the grounds of her manor house.

The Royalist highwaymen, Captain James Hind, Thomas Allen and John Cottington, decided to combine crime with patriotism, assaulting mostly Parliamentarians and sundry anti-monarchists. They once made an attempt on the coach of Oliver Cromwell, but his guards killed Allen and chased Hind and Cottington off. Hind was finally captured at Worcester in 1652. He suffered the dreadful punishment of being hung, drawn and quartered. Gold coins spilled out of his chopped bowels. Cottington was apprehended in 1659. He was luckier in his designated agony. He bribed the judge at his trial and was merely sentenced to be strangled with a cord made from the tails of twelve diseased rats.

The strangest pair of highwaymen to ever circulate around the roads of a perilous England were undoubtedly Guy Halfaface and Double Pugh. In accordance with a neat destiny, they paired up one midnight on Hounslow Heath. Guy lacked most of his skull, having lost it abroad, probably in France. Pugh had a spare one growing out of his shoulder. He was in fact two men in one body, conjoined twins, almost completely superimposed on each other, with just the surplus head to disrupt the alignment. There was no need for Guy to wear a mask: the mass of bandages which held his damaged mind in place was both a disguise and a distinguishing mark. As for Pugh, two masks were necessary.

Both men were unsuccessful at robbery until they found themselves victims of a mutual hold-up. Neither knew where to aim his pistol. They became partners. They shared the hatred of commoners and the mistrust of outlaws. But they operated in tandem for a year, before Guy's bandages were caught in thorns as he rode through undergrowth. They unravelled and his exposed brain was pecked by magpies while he was still in the saddle. Pugh continued alone for another month, but his forgetfulness proved to be his undoing. He neglected to mask his second head. It was later recognised in a tavern and sentenced to be hung. His main head was acquitted due to lack of evidence, but it eventually starved to death as he dangled from the gallows.

Less desperate and more robust, William Davis kept his villainous activities secret from his wife and children. They believed that he was a simple farmer who ploughed all his fields at night with a blunderbuss and cutlass. One fateful evening, after drinking too much ale, he tried to rob a coach with a trowel and bag of carrot seed. He was chained to a post on Bagshot Heath and his clothes were filled with earth and planted with root crops. He was regularly fed and watered by his wife, but within a season he was fully crushed to death by the growing parsnips in his shirt and breeches. Inevitably his corpse was stolen by graverobbers and sold to vegetarian witches in Surrey.

The most glamorous highwayman of all was an import. Claude Duval was born in Normandy and decided to work the roads of England because his accent would charm the female passengers of the coaches he robbed into parting with their jewellery without a fight. He was not mistaken. He quickly earned a reputation as a dancer, singer and kisser, a dandy who charged helpless husbands £100 a time for the privilege of watching him seduce their wives in roadside ditches. Unusually, he retired from the job before the authorities terminated his career for him. Unwisely he chose alchemy as his next profession, and expired after falling into a vat of molten lead which he planned to transmute into gold with the aid of a forged spellbook and a jar of powdered unicorn horn.

The Defaulted Wife

The only highwayman who ever amassed more loot than Thomas Sympson lived half a century later. Unlike 'Old Mobb' he had no compassion or interest in fashion. He was a brute of the utmost gloating, a drooling idiot who yet possessed enough aptitude to arrange a beneficial image for himself. He was born Richard Dick, but he instinctively understood the advantages of pilfering the identities and achievements of other robbers. There was a local highwayman by the name of Dean Pinter who rode a mule instead of a horse and thus enjoyed a brief career. Richard stole his surname and rearranged its two syllables, condemning its original owner to historical oblivion. A misspelling completed the theft. Thus Dick Turpin emerged not from a womb but from his own unthinking head. His first act as an outlaw was to stab the only schoolmaster in his village and abduct his pencils, which he subsequently ate.

The county of Essex was notorious for the low level of education of its citizens. Turpin decided that they were too clever for him and so he moved to London. By the time he arrived, he forgot he was supposed to be a highwayman. He secured employment as a butcher. The man who gave him the job was a smuggler of venison, which was a meat only licensed to the teeth of aristocrats. Turpin was sent into the forests beyond London to kill deer and bring them back hidden beneath cart-loads of vegetables. He discharged his duty admirably but not without a measure of confusion. It later emerged that he attempted to rob the deer before shooting them, demanding that they hand over their purses and gems. On one occasion, he rode back on a deer, with his dead horse in the cart. His employer knew a doctor who agreed to examine Turpin. The diagnosis was 'brain pox' and the recommended cure was the wearing of a hat made from a hedgehog. The patient was not allowed to remove it even in bed. Turpin used it as an extra pocket, impaling small objects on its spines.

In June 1727, returning to his lodgings after work, he lost his way in the fog and entered the wrong house. The woman who lived there was so shocked by the appearance of the dirty rogue she was unable to protest. This condition persisted for the remainder of her life. Dick Turpin was forced to assume he was her husband. There was no other explanation for her existence in his abode. He could not remember the wedding, but that was a minor detail and could be shrugged off. She cooked him a meal and they slept together that night. The bedroom was full of mirrors. In the morning, he rose and tried to demand money off his own reflection. Then perceiving there were more of them than him, he backed away. Perhaps he slipped on a rug. At any rate, he struck his head on the sharp corner of a chair. The result of this blow was temporary amnesia, and a doubling of his intelligence, for he completely forgot he was incompetent. Even so, he remained stupid and vile.

The Lunatic Ride

Exactly a year later, his employer, wealthy on the profits of Turpin's hunting of deer, bought his protégé his own butcher's shop. The gift was received with panic. Turpin understood only that his responsibilities had increased. His initial reaction was to raise money to bribe them to shrink again. Banditry against humans seemed the only answer. He fled with his wife to the marshes of Canvey Island, a desolate region settled by other robbers. One by one he relieved them of their savings. Rumours filtered back to him that he was the most wanted man in England. After sunset, lanterns fixed to long poles carried by men on stilts flickered over the stagnant waters. Bounty hunters were searching for him. Within a month, he amassed enough lamps to open a lantern shop. He dwelled in a reed hut which he built with his own wife's hands. It was illuminated on the inside by wills-o'-the-wisp which flared and moved across his sodden rugs. By this light, she read him books.

In such a fashion, Turpin came to learn of his predecessors in the business. The tale of William Nevison was his favourite. Nevison earned himself the nickname of 'Swift Nick' for one daring exploit. Following a robbery at Gad's Hill, Kent, he galloped all the way to the city of York in fifteen hours. The distance was approximately 200 miles. Considering the average speed of 14 miles per hour for a healthy horse, it is clear that Nevison must have changed steeds many times. Nearly two centuries later, George Osbaldeston, a champion rider, duplicated the feat using no less than 28 different horses. The point of the ride was to exclude Nevison from suspicion. When he was arrested for the robbery in Kent, he called witnesses who swore on oath to have spoken to him on the same day in York. The court judged it impossible for a man to cover the distance between the two locations in so short a time. They acquitted him. It was a ploy which might only work once.

Turpin comprehended nothing of Nevison's reasons for the adventure. He cared only for its superficial excellence. He decided to claim it for his own. He painted his wife with tar, fixed a hairy tail to her rump, ordered her to walk on all fours and started referring to her as 'Black Bess'. Then he led her back to London. She was his horse, he insisted, and had carried him from Kent to York without pausing at all. Although sixty years had passed since Nevison accomplished the stunt for real, the public swallowed Turpin's version of events. Nevison was forgotten. In 1834, the historical novelist, William Harrison Ainsworth, published his first book, *Rookwood*, which supported all Turpin's lies and added a few of its own. This story established him in the public mind as a bold and romantic hero, an outcast only because of social injustices and the corruption of the law. The highwayman once buried a bag of silver coins in a field. Perhaps he guessed that any future writer who found it would regard it as fair payment for a positive literary portrait. Ainsworth's house was constructed on that site.

Yet Another Turpin

Already the toast of London high society for his supposed sophistication and chivalrous qualities, Turpin had a lucky encounter on Putney Heath which enhanced the mirage of his character considerably. He tried to rob another renowned highwayman, Thomas King, who laughed in his face at the irony. The mistake proved advantageous to Turpin. They decided not only to team up, but also to swap identities. King was a genuine hero of the roads, stealing from the rich and giving to the poor, with a modest 25% handling fee. Turpin was an indiscriminate butcher and buffoon. Both were wanted by the authorities. Clearly if King pretended to be Turpin, and Turpin to be King, they might be safe from execution, for they would be arrested, charged, tried and sentenced under incorrect names and thus could not be legally hung. It was an inspired idea. Unaware that Turpin was a brute, King assumed with everybody else he was a dashing hero like himself. The final result of this exchange was a perfect reputation for the monster and an appalling one for the gentleman.

Turpin moved to a second hut in the depths of a forest and emerged only to slaughter travellers who alerted him by breaking dry twigs with the hooves of their mounts. King roamed the whole of England, bowing to ladies and feeding orphans. Turpin licked gore from his hands. King was invited to weddings and birthdays. Turpin dressed in mud and leaves and resolved not to speak in words. King wrote exquisite poetry and sang to a guitar. Turpin rotated all his loose teeth in their sockets until they faced backward and went blind in one eye because he forgot to blink it. His amnesia had worn off. He was better, and thus much worse. King felt there was nothing amiss with men who wore pink, and encouraged families from the poorest countries in the world to emigrate to England, helping them fill in the application forms. Turpin grunted his wife to death. King sniffed flowers. Turpin did not.

Everything now attributed to Turpin was the work of King. The smile and manners, sensitivity and sense of honour. King continued to sanctify the name of Turpin, acting on the misunderstanding that Turpin was doing the same for him. One morning, an hour before dawn, a lone horseman with a sack of gold and food deliberately rode off the designated trail in an isolated wood. Turpin heard the snapping twigs and leaped out of his hut with his blunderbuss. He had brought no shot with him, so he plucked the spines out of his hat and pushed them into the barrel. When the stranger came close, he discharged this weapon directly into his face. The victim did not die immediately. He fell to the ground, gasped that his name was Dick Turpin and that his blood had stopped circulating. "I have pins and needles in both cheeks," he cried. Then he added that he had heard about a very poor man who lived alone in the forest and that he had come with money and cakes as a gift. He said no more.

The real Turpin stood and scratched his head, the first time he had been able to do so without puncturing his fingertips. He decided to look for this poor man in the hut. Perhaps he could rob him. He strode off in a northerly direction, because he had once been told that the north was higher than the south, and he wished to have a clear view of anybody who might be pursuing him. To his surprise, the way was mostly downhill. The hut must have been very elusive or cleverly disguised. After a week, he came to the edge of the forest. His hunger rapidly increased. He saw no reason why he could not catch and cook his own meals. He met a tinker selling kitchen implements. He licked his lips. The entire world can be a hut, he realised, and very poor men are everywhere.

The Jump

Turpin was arrested in October 1738 on the charge of stealing a grouse and trying to boil a saucepan over it. He was deemed mad and his thumbs were severed in an attempt to cure him, for it was widely believed that picking one's nose was the sole cause of insanity. Showing few signs of improvement, he was sentenced to death, together with the grouse, at the end of March 1739. The jury recognised him as the depraved Thomas

King. It was lamented that he had none of the courage, style or decency of the famous Dick Turpin. He slept through most of his execution, awakening in time to jump from the scaffold in order to break his own neck and avoid a slow strangulation. The force was not great enough. It did not matter. He was heard to snore loudly as the mob tugged at his feet to hasten his end. He had fallen asleep again.

The Maddest King
Henri Christophe

Mad

Charles III, Ferdinand I and Francis I of Naples; Charles XII of Sweden; Joseph II of Austria; Frederick I, Frederick William II and Frederick William IV of Prussia; Leopold II of Belgium; George III and George IV of England; Augustus II of Poland; Charles V, Charles VIII, Louis XIV, Louis XV, Louis XVI and Louis XVII of France; Peter III of Russia; Carol II of Romania; Mahomet III, Osman II, Ahmed III, Mahmud I, Murad V and Abdul Hamid II of Turkey; Alexander I of Greece; James II of Scotland; John V of Portugal; Ludwig I of Bavaria.

Madder

Frederick William I of Prussia; Paul I of Russia; Ferdinand I of Austria; Charles VI and Louis XVIII of France; Murad IV of Turkey; Menelik II of Ethiopia; Otto I and Ludwig II of Bavaria; Eric XIV of Sweden; Christian VII of Denmark.

Maddest

Henri Christophe of Haiti.

The Steamy Land

The poorest country in the western hemisphere, suffocated with jungles and choked with magic, humid and mysterious, populated by freed slaves and captive ghosts, with thick mists rolling up its secret mountains, Haiti is only half an island but a whole new world. In sound, its name is connected with loathing. In image, it has a grotesque theatricality which contrives to be both sombre and hot. The players in this mutated drama are the sorcerers garbed like undertakers, the props are the tools of their trade: snakes, drums and living corpses, each with its own rhythm, sinuous or hypnotic or convulsive. The idea that normal life might exist here is far more implausible than the belief that dead men can rise and walk and leer.

The spells of voodoo are complex and dreadful, nets of sound cast high and far and long to attract or trap loose spirits. There is little transparency in the phantoms of this domain. They do not drift or flap on a gentle breeze, or catch and sail the reflected solar wind of a full moon with outstretched arms, ectoplasmic membranes taut as drumskins in the spicy, smoky night. They are not spectres of wisp and rustle. They are invisible, intangible and attenuated only when they are not in this world at all. Unlike ghosts in more developed nations, they do not pass through walls. Nor will they allow themselves to be imprisoned in jars or paintings. For when they arrive, it is always directly into a strong body brimming with blood and bile. They can kick down doors. The spirits of Haiti are entirely physical.

The Chains of Freedom

Only the slaves of Surinam won their liberty before those of Haiti and they were fewer and gentler. The oppressed masses of the magic isle had to fight long and hard for *their* release. The abolitionists who paraded the streets of the cities of the later Americas preferred to claim that their own demonstrations and marches were the one key in the lock which opened the manacles for millions and allowed the prisoners to walk free again.

The truth is that violence rather than enlightenment worked best in the plantations of the Caribbean.

The uprisings of the slaves, which were put down with an astounding savagery, did not diminish in number. They became more frequent. Soon it was more trouble than it was worth for landowners to continue to harvest sugarcane with a reluctant and rebellious workforce. There was no change of faith, no conversion to compassion. There was practical economics and heads lopped silently with oiled sickles. The insurgents had far less to lose than those they struggled against. They went into battle behind the twin symbols of the snake and cross.

The French had taken possession of Haiti in 1697, although colonial settlements founded by the buccaneers of Tortuga already existed in the northwest. It soon became the most prosperous New World colony, renowned for its sugar, coffee, cotton, cocoa, indigo, music and fevers. In 1791, this land surged with ten slaves for every free white man. Influenced by the ideals of the French Revolution, a full rebellion was scheduled for the long steamy night of August 24th. It was successful. The declaration of independence was signed in brandy.

In order to maintain its trading links with the new nation, France abolished slavery in 1794. Haiti remained without a ruler until a slave by the name of Toussaint-L'Ouverture appointed himself governor in order to deal with foreign powers. The French demanded to see the declaration of independence. It was a suspicious request. Fearing they might destroy this piece of paper and throw history into doubt that the revolution had occurred, Toussaint immediately concealed it in the least read volume on a random shelf in a minor library of Port-au-Prince, his capital. Ironic rumour insists that it was a book on etiquette or subterfuge. Eventually it was borrowed but never returned.

The French grew restless and annoyed with this insolence. Napoleon sent his cousin, General Charles Leclerc, with a force to restore the old regime and reintroduce slavery. The invasion of Haiti cost many lives on both sides, but eventually Toussaint offered to make a truce. This was accepted and he was invited onto Leclerc's flagship. The following act of betrayal was highly symbolic. Toussaint was clamped in irons and cast into the hold. A sickle was placed just out of his reach. When the ship reached France, he was imprisoned and allowed to starve to death. He had never learned to communicate with spirits. The black rulers of Haiti who followed would not make the same mistake.

The Choked Cannons

France now believed it had regained the colony. Napoleon decided to give Leclerc his deserved rest and appointed the Viscount de Rochambeau to take over the humbled nation. The followers of Toussaint saw their chain returning over the waves, ready to fix them to a distant master. By the time the foreign fleet reached port, a thousand Haitians were waiting to greet them with muskets and daggers. The Viscount ordered the discharge of a cannon into the crowd. It misfired and exploded inside the ship. A blaze was soon raging out of control and the barrels of gunpowder in the hold began to detonate. The Viscount and a handful of sailors managed to lower a longboat and escape. A second, third and fourth ship fired their guns but these also exploded. The remainder of the fleet turned around and sailed for home, the Viscount cursing and bellowing as his men rowed after them. Haiti was free again.

Emerging from the water and climbing onto the wooden dockside with some assistance, an outlandish figure stumbled into the arms of friends. This was a man in a crude, experimental diving suit. The glass helmet with fitted snorkel was removed and he was permitted to catch his breath before being carried on the shoulders of the mob through the streets. He was young and muscular with perfect teeth but his hair was prematurely white. He spoke fluent English as well as French and explained that none of his comrades had survived the mission. They had drowned on the swim home. He was taken to a brothel where the girls rewarded him for a month without payment. He was not a talkative customer but his story quickly spread: a small group of brave divers had secretly boarded the invading vessels the previous night and interfered with every cannon. How they achieved this sabotage was never specified, but there were hints it involved magic.

The Treacle of Temerity

Henri Christophe was born on the neighbouring island of Grenada. He was the only son of slaves brought over by the British from West Africa to toil in the sugarcane fields. The tribe from which he was descended was famous for its stubborn nature, aggression and determination to resist any form of captivity. Henri embodied all these qualities to excess. He caused so much trouble on the plantations that his master finally sold him to a passing sea captain as a cabin boy. The captain rapidly learned that Henri's obstinacy could not be broken by the usual punishments. He eventually grew weary of ordering the boy to be flogged and decided to sell him to a plantation owner on the island of Hispaniola. This was a time when Spanish control of the western side of the island had been fatally weakened by the French, who practised an even more extreme brand of colonial depravity and cynicism.

Henri realised his sufferings in Grenada had been mild compared with those of this new province, named Haiti after a word of its (extinct) original inhabitants which meant "land of strange mountains". He believed he was certain to be shot or hung by the plantation owner, for he found it impossible to tame his natural audacity and will to resist. His rescue came from a war in a distant country. The United States of America declared its independence from the British Empire. France, seeing an opportunity to be revenged on an old enemy, provided munitions and recruits to the American cause. Some of the most willing volunteers came from the Black populations of the French Caribbean. One morning a recruiting officer visited the plantation where Henri worked. His master had little choice but to let him go. Fighting the British was considered the patriotic duty of every Frenchman. Henri made three vows as he walked out of the plantation. The first was never to return and to forget all about his past. The second was to return as soon as possible and revenge himself on his former master. The third was to do both. This was the one he favoured. Throughout life he never allowed contradictions or impossibilities to trouble him.

The Direct Hit

In the misty forests of Vermont and New Hampshire, Henri distinguished himself as a man with almost no fear, shooting soldiers in scarlet coats with startling accuracy (and staining those jackets an even darker red) and living easily off the land. He befriended another Haitian volunteer, Jean-Jacques Dessalines, and together they discussed the possibility of freedom for their own country. Henri often complained of headaches but never allowed pain to interfere with his performance. It was obvious to Dessalines that his new comrade was mad, but with a shrug of his broad shoulders he concluded it was none of his business. One morning, seeking provisions in a house on the shores of Lake Winnipesaukee, they chanced on a skeleton in a curious outfit. It was a prototype diving suit. The dead owner had been an eccentric and reclusive inventor. Henri and Dessalines examined the suit to fathom its secrets, dragging it outside to the lake and testing it in the waters. They took turns to reach the bottom. Dessalines went first and reported seeing only boring weeds and bored fish through the helmet. Henri claimed to have observed other divers swimming past.

Over a bottle of fine requisitioned brandy (the inventor was a man of taste) the two men decided to report this find to the commander of their unit. The following morning they set off back to base. Within one mile of their destination they were ambushed by British snipers. Henri received a bullet in the head — the ball bounced off his skull but an area the size of a child's fist had been shattered. Throwing him over his shoulder, Dessalines made his escape. Henri raved in hospital until a surgeon cut away the splintered bone. The injury was not fatal. It was possible to live with a perforated cranium, provided one avoided magpies and immersion. Henri quickly recovered and went back to war. The British yolk was cast off and the freedom of the United States was established.

During this time, both men neglected to tell anyone else about their discovery of the diving suit. Finally they agreed to keep it a secret and make use of it for their own future campaigns. Returning to Haiti, they witnessed the betrayal of Toussaint. In basement workshops in Port-au-

Prince, craftsmen toiled to create copies of the futuristic outfit. Despite the warnings about immersion, Henri insisted on testing the first model. It seemed to be airtight. Haiti was declared independent a second and final time on the first day of the year 1804. It was generally expected that Henri would be elected president, but he was too busy with his prostitutes. The country remained without a ruler until October, when an exasperated Dessalines assumed the title emperor.

The Sweet Anointing

The removal of a circle of skull to release pressure on the brain is an ancient and valid surgical procedure known as trepanation. The hole in Henri's head cured his headaches, which were symptoms of his insanity, but did nothing to soothe the toxic ideas beneath. Those still pulsed in his exposed brain. Had Dessalines not been killed in a mulatto revolt in 1806, this insanity would have remained in one mind and not infected an entire country. The circumstances of this tragedy are simple and sticky. Haiti was split into two, a northern and southern republic, because the two best friends of Dessalines, Henri himself and a man called Alexandre Sabès Pétion, had both been named as the late emperor's heirs. Dice were cast and Henri was given the north.

For ten years both men ruled reasonably, improving the economies of their territories, building schools, raising their citizens to a level of literacy unequalled in the Caribbean. Pétion was undeniably sane, Henri was clearly mad, but their actions were almost identical. Pétion's sanity was tolerated by those around him, although he was severely introverted, because his political decisions were beneficial. Henri's madness was tolerated by those around him, although he was severely extroverted, because his political decisions were beneficial. One barely whispered at frugal dinners, the other ranted his way through a dozen courses. The officials of Pétion's government gossiped about his sanity behind his back and this gossip was almost interchangeable with that of Henri's officials when they shared anecdotes about his madness. In spite of being so similar, or because of it, relations between the two rulers finally deteriorated. War was declared. Historians are divided on the question whether this was a civil war or not. There were two independent countries, both bearing the name Haiti. Henri believed it *was* a civil war. He also believed it was not.

Another of his beliefs at that time was that republics should never declare war on each other. He decided to resign his presidency and crown himself king. Now the north was a kingdom and no longer had to aspire to be democratic in any way. Henri was free to rule without justifying his orders. He commanded his troops to wear diving suits and swim along rivers into the south, armed with tridents. They refused. Henri realised his authority as a king was not yet sanctioned by tradition. He arranged a coronation. To draw attention to his country's main export, he had himself anointed with chocolate syrup instead of scented oil. The priest who conducted the ritual was so nervous he emptied the entire jug of syrup over his king's head. Not a single drop trickled down the regal face. Henri blinked and then remembered the hole in his head. The chocolate quickly soaked into his brain. He fell down in a fattening stupor. Within a week he had recovered but there was an unhealthy light in his eyes. Suddenly all his orders seemed sensible. The troops swam off in waves. It was the monsoon season. The rains came and the rivers swelled. His entire fleet of mermen were swept over waterfalls or dashed against trees in flooded forests.

MADMAN IN A HIGH CASTLE

The war came to a stalemate. The sides were too evenly matched. Fearing for the security of his country, Henri embarked on a program of castle building. He imported architects from Europe and toyed with the idea of creating an undersea castle in the shape of a giant diving suit. Nothing he suggested ever seemed odd to people near him. Only beyond a radius of perhaps fifty miles from his presence did anyone question his wisdom and competence. Foreign dignitaries reported the weird experience of a visit to King Henri. At first, warned by rumour, they sailed toward Haiti in trepidation, convinced they had been sent to deal with an incurable lunatic. Then, landing in port, they began wondering exactly how mad he would turn out to be. Surely he could not be *that* bad? On the journey to his palace of Sans Souci, through opaque jungle and invisible drumbeats, they were already half certain that stories of his madness had been unfairly exaggerated. Finally, when they beheld him for real, the sudden realisation came upon them that he was the sanest man alive. Departing back to their own countries, this process took place in reverse. It seemed that Henri was a man who was able to contaminate others with his delusions. His daftness was contagious.

When Pétion died from natural causes in 1818, Henri was able to end the war and unite the two parts of Haiti into a single state. Few people in the south complained. They were too busy with the required number of books to be read each year — education had become a legal duty of every citizen. Indeed it was a punishable offence *not* to study. Henri did not repeal this law. He changed almost nothing of Pétion's administration, because it was practically identical to his own. But the castle building continued. Now he felt threatened by the Spanish, who were desperate to halt the recent reversal of their fortunes in the Americas. Forcing his architects to work without sleep for a week, he soon had the plans of the most imposing (and dreamlike) fortress in the world. The Citadelle Laferrière was constructed in the shape of a ship on the peak of a mountain overlooking Cap-Haïtien more than three thousand feet above the level of the sea. Then he armed the citadel with enormous guns, which had to be dragged up a steep winding path. Some 20,000 men died from exhaustion before the final gun was in place. None complained. Some observers remarked that the castle bore no resemblance to a ship. They felt a more accurate comparison was a man in a bizarre helmet swimming through the sky.

One Typical Act of Madness

Henri decided that only the most loyal troops might be relied upon to effectively protect Haiti from invasion. But how could he decide who he should trust? He ordered his entire army to march over the parapet of the Citadelle Laferrière. All those who obeyed fell to their deaths, all who refused were executed on the spot. Henri now knew who he could trust. The dead soldiers at the bottom of the mountain were conscripted into a special new force. Perhaps he believed his voodoo skills might reanimate them. Legions of pulped men guarded his palaces, castles and chocolate processing plants.

The Sealed Head

As well as architects and teachers, Henri also imported foreign doctors. One of these was Giovanni Barzini, a surgeon from Italy with many modern ideas on the subject of insanity. He examined Henri and concluded that the king's madness was actually bigger than his mind. It was an utterly unique case. Normally it would not be a problem: the huge madness would remain locked inside the skull, building up pressure but not infecting anyone else, but with the hole in Henri's head, it was able to expand outwards, enveloping all those in his vicinity in an invisible bubble of insanity. His subjects shared his madness and were willing to do anything he said, because to them it seemed logical and sane.

The cure was simple. Barzini made a wax plug the same size as the hole and sealed Henri's head. Now the madness was locked away. Henri was still totally mad but his subjects recovered their reason. Henri took his first bath since the American War of Independence. He assumed that immersion was permitted to him again. As he dipped his head under the hot water, the wax plug melted. Suddenly the chocolate sauce which had been trapped in his brain since his coronation was released. It rose to the surface of the bath like a slick. It seemed almost like a false alchemist's trick! Henri's madness was no longer bigger than his mind. It was small enough for him to understand that sane madmen should kill themselves. He jumped out of the bath and found a pistol in his bedroom. There was no need to pull the trigger. There was already a hole in his skull. He just needed to ram the barrel of the pistol inside very hard. His brave dead soldiers proved no use in preventing his citizens from entering his palace in the spirit of revolution and dancing around his cadaver.

STREETCORNER MOUSE

To Gabriel Mesa

Streetcorner Mouse

Fancy you coming here and asking me whether I ever knew Tin Dylan. The answer is that I met him once. A bad bard, he was. The folks he offended were real musicians, and he hurt them with his harp. Strung with cheap wires, that implement, the same way his forehead was marked with bargain wrinkles. Couldn't even do a proper frown with five lines to smudge the notes on with a dirty thumb. That's how we play it down our way. We love tunes and dancing and take unkindly to anybody who doesn't do it right. Dylan was one of those who couldn't manage it. He wasn't from our town. Told us he'd come from Kenfig Pool just outside Porthcawl to the west. I misunderstood him at first and thought he meant he'd emerged from under the pool, which would account for his slimy character, but it turns out he hadn't. Not that you could tell the difference. He smelled like dirty water and his clothes were like weeds. There was no shape on him at all, but he acted like a fresh article*. He strolled into the pub without even a blink and didn't seem perturbed by the abrupt silence. Nobody in their proper mind does that in the middle of our territory, and for a moment I wondered if he had a special type of courage or sadness. But we soon got to learn how daft he truly was.

Not easy to credit, but the tale of that night — a night untidy as any under a roof — started just before Dylan entered. The guitarist who ought to have been twanging his tunes hadn't turned up. I was trying to persuade Bronwen to dance with me anyhow, but she didn't know the steps to silence. A vile pub, THE TALL STORY, and one of the worst holes ever filled with rabble instead of rubble. Bronwen was typical of the ladies who went there. There were mystical innuendoes in nearly everything she said. The other girls were arcane and erudite, but Bronwen had them all beat.

* A 'fresh article' is Wenglish for a stylish and confident man.

I like my women to be eldritch. Some fellows I know prefer to have them thaumaturgical. That'll do for me too. Those eyebrows of hers were joined and crepuscular. I kept staring at them as I asked her again and again for a spin on the floor. They were so thick and heavy she couldn't lift them to indicate doubt or surprise. That really softened my heart, I'll tell you. Even when she pulled a knife on me, I was more transfixed by that hairy horizon on her face than by the cold steel of her refusal. I wouldn't leave her alone, and I think she would have murdered me with a flick of her wrist if the door hadn't opened and the hard shadow of a long man fallen right between us.

It acted like a shield, that shadow, which was odd, for they don't usually have any substance to them. The blade hissed as Bronwen sheathed it reluctantly. The newcomer wasn't Dylan yet. He wiped a wet belch from his chin with his sleeve and strutted to the bar. He called for a drink. Hywel the barman passed him a full bottle of brandy for free, because he didn't look the kind to pay gently. Then someone nudged me and whispered that this was Big Llygoden Fach, the Jew's-harp player, and that he was always looking for a duet. A Jew's-harp didn't strike me as being the wisest instrument to bring to one of our dances, which are about volume as much as melody, but I decided to hold my tongue. My own speciality is the steam organ and I'd left mine at home. I'm retired from that game. I prefer to listen to the young men hurling their notes at each other now. It's less effort. Stomping the dancefloor seems more sensible at my age, which is the same as yours, I guess. You wouldn't take a steam organ to a pub, would you? Llygoden hadn't even displayed his instrument, but we were all baffled and anxious. Then he drained off the bottle, turned his tiny eyes on all of us and said:

"The guitarist will never make it. Met him down the next alley from here. Thought he was a cool cat, he did, and I had to utterly change his mind. Not nice to leave you all quiet on the dancing front, so I decided to take his place. He was handy practice, but now I'm looking for a real musician to form a new duo. I heard there might be a player here skilled enough to teach me — me being nobody, you understand — some new tricks of the stave. He's the one I want to meet. A strummer, blower or plinker I can accompany. A man of talent."

He made that speech, and never took his eyes off us. His gaze was a sharp one, we agreed later, and I felt scrammed over the jib. But nobody answered him, not even to call out in pain from that jagged look of his, and the pub went even more quiet than quiet, which is to say silent, for there is a vast difference between quiet and silent, same way portentous and pretentious might seem identical from some angles, but aren't. Never had THE TALL STORY acted so timid, with even the rafters and windows and pony brasses on the walls, which don't ordinarily have lungs, seeming to hold their breath, not that they have any, but they do have the absorbed odours of tired centuries which pass for it. You could have heard an ear drop, a soft one at that, all flaky and bloated, into a jug of beer with a comfy head, the same as what Bronwen did to that pig fellow who made a grunting pass at her last summer. I drank that right down, because I was desperate to impress her, but it didn't work. Tasted of toast, it did. A lady who is supremely disdainful can't be won even with such sacrifices, but I keep trying all the same. Silk purses have nothing on her soul for luxurious depth, but at the bottom of *her* inner void are only grim dooms waiting. Reach in anyway, I will.

The silence continued, until I started to believe we were all fleas or something else that is born deaf, and then the door opened again. And this time it was Dylan with his harp. Like a lath, he was, his talent, I mean, which is to say very thin, but we only guessed that at this point, because it seemed logical, and later we knew for certain. Anyhow, he had no awareness of the awkwardness in his surroundings, but just strode in, not blinking his eyes, which were nothing like Llygoden's, and reaching the bar right next to the challenger he rested his harp on its varnished surface and tactlessly announced:

"I have no money, but they let me pay with songs."

Just then I felt something pushing against my leg and I realised it was Bronwen moving forward to get a better look. I enjoyed this contact and was grateful to the newcomer for inspiring it, even as I scorned his idiocy. Because Hywel made no move, Dylan reached out and coaxed a minor chord from his harp with a thumb and three fingers. I wanted to chuckle, because the sound was feeble, even dirty in an odd way, but I controlled myself. The room was agape at his temerity and Llygoden just smouldered and twitched by his side, but Dylan was clearly unaware of the danger he was in, and he blithely added:

"Strung with tin, it is, to preserve the songs of legend. Stops 'em going off into modern variations."

And he smiled to himself so smugly that I knew none who watched him would feel much sympathy whatever was done to him, which was going to be lots, and all nasty, or so it seemed. For when Hywel didn't give him the drink he wanted, Dylan simply reached out and grabbed Llygoden's bottle of brandy, knocking it back winky* and licking his blubbery lips with the air of a man pretending to be used to a superior vintage. His harp still hummed on the bar, and the whispers of sound were like the sighing of the bugs in his clothes as they anticipated having to abandon his body, because in a few minutes it would be cold and leaking. And we all shared their imaginary opinion on this issue. The one mystery remaining was why Llygoden hadn't finished him off already. Maybe he wasn't so sure that Dylan really was an imbecile. Perhaps he thought he was acting. I reckon it was because he wanted to make an example of this upstart to the whole gathering, to prove to us that he was something to be respected not just tonight, when he was actually around, but even behind his shadow, in the wake of that unyielding smear.

Dylan finished the bottle and started picking his teeth, though it was plain he hadn't eaten anything for days, because that's the look he had, with the feverish, pious light in his eyes that ascetics have when they can't position their haloes anywhere else. It was probably decayed enamel he was scraping off with his long fingernails. Then I noticed how the strings of his harp were threaded with black blobs and I calculated there was nearly a mouthful of rotten teeth on the wires, from where he had transferred his jaw pickings by neglecting to wash his hands before playing. Strange thing is, they looked like quavers and crotchets fixed there, and some mutated notes nobody ever sounded before. So he had bad music even as an accidental effect of his bad habits. This made me think he was destined to be involved with songs, that fate desired him to make melodies, however awful, and that we shouldn't mock him too cruelly, in case

* Winky = with a rapid and smooth motion.

we offended the Muse of Sound, to whom we all owed allegiance. Then again, maybe he was just plain disgusting and needed to visit a dentist. That was the preferred option.

All that aside, it was now Llygoden's turn to speak again, and he issued a challenge, as I assumed he would, and he did it in a legato and dangerous voice, then his lean hand strayed to the pocket where he kept his instrument. Bronwen pushed harder into me, but there was no need for her to move that much closer, for even those at the far back of the room heard him croon the following:

"So you're the one, are you? The man who can give me a real duet. I crave satisfaction on this score."

Now Dylan blinked innocent eyes and replied: "I play from memory in the old style and I never read music from scores, but I'll try anything once, and if I don't already know it I'll pick it up after just a single demonstration, if you please."

Before I could stop her, Bronwen moved forward and walked right up to Dylan, slipping her knife out and handing it to him. I was aghast at the way she always liked to make trouble.

"I think you're going to need this."

Dylan took it and turned it over in his hand. He seemed astonished by the blade and the fact there wasn't the slightest trace of blood on it. He frowned and shook his head.

"Don't fight with weapons, me, but with music, like my ancestors. All bards are exempt from combat."

She glared at him. "It's to slide the notes."

Llygoden gave her an appreciative look and slapped her behind with his eyes and mind, which she didn't feel or didn't care, I'm not certain which, and he said: "We're going to do it Hawaiian style, are we? Or is it the Blues you're angling for?"

"Know the Hawaiian Blues, I do," blurted Dylan.

"Two knives you'll need for that," called out someone, and I think it was Hywel, which meant THE TALL STORY was coming alive again and this new situation had become part of the evening's entertainment. And others began shouting mildly pointless comments, just to be heard and to prove they still existed and had courage.

"In a shield there's two knives' worth!"

"A shadow is worth three shields..."

"In a chest there's four shadows' worth!"

"A stairs is worth five chests..."

"In a spring there's six stairs' worth!"

"A summer is worth seven springs..."

And so on, none of it making much sense, but spoken mostly for the rhythms of the words rather than for any meaning. The sequence faded out before the count reached a hundred.

Then Llygoden leaned right close to Dylan and asked: "Do you want to get changed before we commence?"

And Dylan answered: "I'm on form now."

The sound of eyebrows rising throughout the pub, with the exception of Bronwen's singular and immobile one, was caused by a displacement of air towards the ceiling. We roared:

"On form now? So what were you before?"

And Dylan declared: "Not as good as what I am."

This reply was disturbing in the extreme. Rattled, it had us. Now I saw that everybody had Dylan marked down as a trickster, a professional twpsyn, who pretended to be dull but was really very deadly. When a man who obviously can't do anything declares he was even worse before, logic dictates he's bending the truth to snapping point. That's unsettling. It was too late for Llygoden to back down, and I don't think he would have done whatever the circumstances. He wasn't the sort to capitulate. Plus he didn't know for certain what Dylan meant, and only Hywel gave voice to the unlikely idea by asking:

"He's a were-liar, this one, is he?"

"Never heard of that before," somebody muttered.

Llygoden silenced the murmuring by raising a finger to his lips. I saw that his other hand was still in the region of his pocket. He pulled out his Jew's-harp and held it up so that it caught the light of the dim lamps. There wasn't the slightest trace of spit on it. He made a gesture towards his new opponent which was unmistakable and his thumb toyed with the steel band which ran across the centre of his instrument, though it was in no mouth yet and made only a thin sound. In a sudden eruption of bravado, he declared his intention of starting the duet without changing himself, so that Dylan would have the obvious advantage. This suggestion put him back on the summit of our awe. Never had an unchanged man played against one fully transformed, whatever the ultimate shape of the other. Llygoden would go down in local legend if he won the duet. It was quite something to be there at the time.

"Where's there a liar?" blinked Dylan, acting like he was ignorant of everything. "Shall we ask him?"

"Just play," snapped Llygoden, and he jammed his instrument into his maw like he was choking on it.

His thumb resembled the longest hair of a prolapsed nostril blowing in a tempest as it struck the metal bar of the Jew's-harp, so fast that it became a host of petrified afterimages, until it looked like hundreds of thousands of thumbs trying to hitch lifts between all the dimensional layers of the multiverse, unsuccessfully as it turned out, for Llygoden remained with us in ours. But that was the effect. And his tunes matched it, the Music not only of our Spheres, but of others from new realities, some of them not even round. Strange music, and funky. Lunatic arpeggios of shimmering notes, vibrating quicker and quicker, but not necessarily increasing in pitch. It was a music which wove a web with loose ends, a net with frayed corners which spliced themselves into the frayed ends of our unwinding nervous systems, until we the audience became both trapper and victim. Or something like that.

Dylan seemed taken aback by the display. But he knew he had to join in fast or be disqualified from the duet. So he struck an uncertain note on his lowest string. It didn't mix with Llygoden's song, if I may call it that, at all, but the maestro used it to form a chord which was right for the beginning of a variation on his ultracosmic theme. Dylan plucked another note, equally inappropriate, and Llygoden took this as a prompt for a second variation. Dylan's playing was all over the place, totally unstructured and incompetent, but Llygoden *made it right*. He took each mistake as a foundation for a new variation and thus rendered it correct with hindsight, or hindhearing, if I may be permitted that neologism. So in a sense, whatever Dylan played was transmuted by Llygoden's oral and steel alchemy into something he could not do. That was clever. That was unique. That was a winning tactic, for sure. But I failed to discern any Hawaiian or Blues influence in the developing tune. Not that it mattered or that this was part of the rules.

Some of the older patrons of THE TALL STORY, ever since it became a regular venue for our sort of show, had witnessed many duets between all kinds of musicians. They still whispered anecdotes about Deaf Lime Jaffa and his frying pan guitar which had mushrooms and soy sauce in it while he played. And they told tales of Soulless Tony Smith's Jazz Messengers who had harmonic signals to deliver but never managed it, losing them in the first dark improvised passage. And one of our most notorious legends concerned Grampa Chaff who played his own bruises better with a zinc mallet. These champions of the past were fine in their day, but none came close to competing with what we watched now. Llygoden was playing the gig of his, ours and the pub's life, not to mention that of Dylan's death and the contempt of his bones. It was more than a duet. It was a massacre. It should have been horrid to behold, but uplifting it was, especially because we weren't on the other end of the virtuoso display. A relief to realise that. But I don't think Dylan guessed for a moment how violently and deliciously he was losing.

Now Llygoden was entering the final phase of his performance. With a sly wink at the entire fabric of spacetime, he increased the velocity of his thumb. It became invisible. Even the molten afterimages were now travelling faster than the eye. Then his single thumb came back into the focus of my bedazzled vision. It was swelling. I understood slowly what was happening. As an object gradually approaches the speed of light, its mass increases. It takes more and more energy to accelerate it even just a fraction. Physics, that is. Llygoden puffed his cheeks and the sweat sprayed from the pores of his skin, diluting our beer, though the front line of observers stood ten feet or more from the duet. That's how much effort he was putting into this crescendo. The music he mouthed became metaphysical, beyond our comprehension. It seemed to already exist above and behind and within everything. It was indescribable, so I won't try, even with elaborate metaphors. Then it was over, vanished. We were left with a savage emptiness, as if we had lost the most precious thing we'd ever owned, which was our complacency. Llygoden suddenly silenced the Jew's-harp with his tongue and then beamed at us. He looked real jocose. Turning to Dylan he held out his hand for a submissive kiss, but instead of falling on his knees and performing this act of homage, the minimum needed to earn him a painless death, the best he could now hope for, the loser took it in his own hand, shook it curtly and yawned. Then he used this hand to scratch himself in an unmentionable place. When the lunatic deed was done, he enquired:

"Have we finished warming up yet?"

The Jew's-harp dropped out of Llygoden's mouth. This was not just the result of his amazement and anger. It was also because the shape of his jaw was changing. It could no longer hold the instrument. His whole face was becoming more pointed. It was like a smart shoe. It was like a short carrot. Dylan's arrogance had set him off. He was a being of pure instinct now, lacking pity.

I asked nobody in particular: "Any notion what Llygoden is when he changes? I haven't been told."

Bronwen was standing by my side and she answered: "The guitarist we booked was a were-cat. Llygoden defeated him. So he's something fiercer and bigger than a cat. A dog?"

"Maybe a bear or alligator?" offered Hywel.

"Something with a pointy face," I remarked, as I continued to watch the transformation. "Vulture?"

"Not that. He hasn't got a beak."

"Whatever it is, it'll be worse for Dylan."

"Yes, look at his reaction..."

Dylan was retreating with his own face twisted into a snarl. But he wasn't changing into anything. He'd already done that, by his admission. But now he acted like he didn't know the score, which was against him, and for a moment I wondered if he had wandered in here without realising that THE TALL STORY was a shapeshifters' pub, patronised by were-things. But nobody could be so ignorant. He was a were-liar. That was his form. It was an unusual category, to be sure, but that didn't mean it wasn't a valid one. The fact is that he'd lost and now was trying to preserve his life like a coward. He was pointing at Llygoden and shaking with terror and surprise and bawling aloud:

"Grief! A mouse, he is! A mouse!"

And so he was. But no ordinary mouse. Six feet high at least, with a leer that could have frightened a cheese at the distance of the moon. His whiskers were aerials attuned to the wavelength of sneaky menace and scuttling jeebies. Llygoden was a special kind of rodent, an *ubermouse*, such as what they maybe had back in the days before humans. He was the first prehistoric were-thing we'd ever seen. His eyes were still tiny, compared with the rest of his head, but big compared with ours, and I don't think any of us could have poked one properly with our whole arm. As for his two front teeth, it is best not to chatter about those. Nor his ears. And his hairless tail was like an enormous worm in the guts of our shock. It undulated there, and whipped the walls, and coiled around some of our feet. And it strangled a table leg or two, and that was also new, watching furniture dying from lack of oxygen, which was the same breath held by the rafters and windows and pony brasses: aromas from the past, mixed with spilled drinks.

Leaning towards Dylan, so that his wet twitching nose rested on the fool's chest, Llygoden squeaked:

"The only reason I don't chew you up right now is because you make me sick. Worse than pest poison."

At that, Bronwen left my side again and stepped forward and threw both her arms around that furry neck, and she even managed to raise that eyebrow of hers in an appreciative squint, though no more than a tenth of an inch, and she sighed, hotly: "Forget that untidy* bard — he had us thinking he was a smart liar."

Llygoden stood there perplexed for a second, and then he nuzzled right up to her like it was going to be for all eternity, and he yelled at us to play something, even if without instruments, and then he yelled at the rest of us to dance, even if without ankles, which he'd be sure to bite off if we didn't, which is something in the manner of being one of those self-fulfilling predictions we have in such abundance down our way. Llygoden danced like a huge vermin, which was in keeping with what he was, but

* In Wenglish "untidy" means incompetent or evil.

he didn't keep any shadow between his body and Bronwen, now he knew he could get away with it, for although her other shape was that of a wolf, his bulk was too big even for her fangs. They danced right to the door and then passed through.

"Make way, fellows, she's all mine now."

That's what he squeaked, and they went out cheek to cheek, like in a horrible surgical accident with a needle and thread, which happens not too often, but not too rarely neither.

I felt deeply ashamed of myself. I spun around the room a few times on my own, and then dropped myself, complaining about the heat and mob, and I picked my way through the glum dancers and went out. It was still night, but for how long? Well, until dawn, of course, but how beautiful would that phenomenon be now? Not very, spoiled as it was by my loss of Bronwen, not that I'd ever watched the sunrise with her, but it had been within the realms of future possibility until that big mouse had won her away. I hoped to find a stone and smash at least one streetlight just to make myself feel less impotent. I peered down at the ground and right at that moment, someone elbowed me, and it was a relief. Actually it wasn't an elbow, but the corner of a harp. It was Dylan, coming out of the pub all shaken and shandivang*, a real mess bigger than the mess he'd been in when he did first enter, namely total to the power of total, a mess that had never before been calculable.

"Always in the way, you," he snarled. Maybe he was trying to growl away some of his embarrassment. He headed off east, along the quayside, out of town. Never saw him again.

I lurked there looking at my surroundings, the exterior of the pub and its environment, and the building works across the way, and I felt strongly that I was just another leftover in need of redevelopment like all the old parts of this city. The street I was on, Raconteur Road, had always seemed to fit perfectly into its own reputation, right along its length from quay to pink corner, but now it felt out of place, unable to look after itself, even senile. Then I told myself it wasn't like that, for the city might be a were-thing of its own, just changing more slowly than its

* The worst possible psychological condition.

organic equivalent, transforming from a blackspot to a shining capital of the future, whenever that finally turned up. It had promised itself to me for so long now that I'd got tired of waiting each day for it, only to be disappointed it was the present yet again. THE TALL STORY was visibly vibrating with the feet of the dancers inside, and I wanted that to count for something. I struggled to make myself feel no sense of loss over Bronwen, but Llygoden's arrogance, however justified, wouldn't leave me alone. That tall son of a mouse had gotten himself my woman for the night, and maybe for every night, because Bronwen was a cure for all feelings of belatedness. It was impossible to feel you were missing out on anything when she was in your arms, or rather when you were in hers, and her eyebrow was standing in for the edge of the world, beyond which you'd fall into the void of eternal heartache, that infinity where I was stuck now, and mighty uncomfortable there too, I might add. I guess she was stroking that rodent's fur right now, in the first open sewer they'd come to. It was a stinking image.

When I got back inside the pub, the dancers hadn't paused, although they had no need to continue now.

Making myself as inconspicuous as possible, I moved to the bar and ordered a drink from Hywel. He told me that Llygoden had forgotten to take his shadow with him, that protective shield which would have made it impossible for him to enjoy Bronwen anyway. It was stored behind the bar now in case he came back for it. I pretended I wasn't aware of what Hywel was talking about. Sure, I was expecting something to happen, but not what actually did, which was a voice from outside and the sounds of a lady crying, but not with tears. Baying is probably a better word: at a moon which wasn't in the sky, but in a heart. That's supposed to be a romantic figure, but it doesn't work.

"Go in and get me a drink," the voice squeaked, then it grew more desperate. "A large brandy, I need!"

At that, the door opened and Bronwen loped in, though she was still in the form of a woman, only her mannerism had changed, as if she'd just witnessed something gory which had awakened her were-withal, as we call it our way, but hadn't shuffled the atoms of her body, keeping an ace up her spirit's sleeve, so that the deal wouldn't be raw-skin, and then she reached Hywel and myself, and with the lips of a lady but the voice of a wolf, she demanded another bottle.

Hywel was about to fetch one, when Llygoden entered in person, wet nose twitching more slowly now. "I forgot my shadow," he said, and then as he turned, we noticed the marks on his fur. Something had smashed him across the back, breaking his spine. It looked as if he'd been struck by the bar of a gargantuan Jew's-harp. But he was a tough old mouse, that one, and not quite dead yet. Nearly. Then he collapsed and someone said aloud that Bronwen had done it. We all surrounded her at this, probably to give her the credit, but my pride wouldn't stay down, and I pushed my way to her side and wrenched open her mouth with my bare hands, so that her teeth glimmered under the lamps.

"Look at this woman's jaw," I said with a sneer. "It's still human. And even if it was fully lupine, do you think it could open wide enough to bite a giant mouse's back in two?"

Then I added, cool but tough at the same time:

"Who'd have thought that such a clever rodent, able to play a Jew's-harp like nobody ever did, would have ended up this way, in a modest old shapeshifters' pub in Cardiff Docks, where nothing much happens with the exception of a few impossible events now and again, unless a stranger or two enters with an ear for discord?"

Chins were rubbed all round, and drinks ordered the same way. They didn't know if I was blaming Dylan for the killing. I wasn't, but I had worded it badly. It was my own fault.

Just then came the sound of the pub itself changing. It alternated between being a pub for shapeshifters, which is how I always described it, and one for normal folk, which is something I preferred not to think about. This is quite common really. More pubs are were-pubs than you may credit. It was best to get rid of Llygoden's corpse now, because to have it rotting here when the ordinary drinkers came in later would cause all sorts of problems. I think some fellows dragged it outside and dumped it in an alley for the cats. They plucked out most of his whiskers first, as replacement stings for their guitars and mandolins. They were daring enough with a helpless dead mouse. As a trophy they might have cut off his tail as well. I don't know. I didn't follow. Hywel wouldn't take his eyes off me. Bronwen took advantage of this coming and going to vanish, ashamed she'd chosen the wrong side.

People lingered to refine what had happened in words and to sharpen it into an anecdote for future nights. Easy as can be, I left the pub. I heard Hywel discussing me in a low tone as I left. He was gossiping with another patron about my own shape. What sort of a were-thing was I? They agreed that they'd never seen me change. I increased my pace when I knew this was their topic, I can tell you. I didn't want to have to lie. Dawn was coming again, but this time it really had the future harnessed after it. That's what it looked like to me. I'm an optimist, I guess. I walked to my apartment block and looked up at my room. A bottle of oil stood in the window. I decided it was about time I lubricated myself again. Can't say anybody would ever believe in such a being as a were-mousetrap. Made my secret safe. But I didn't want to jam, because I might find myself in that position again. Maybe Llygoden had brothers to avenge him. I put my hand inside my jacket — here by the left armpit, where it always sticks out of my normal shape — and felt the end of my spring. It was just as powerful as before, full of potential energy, and hadn't been stretched by its recent use. And there wasn't the slightest trace of rust on it.

ET AL

To Jeff VanderMeer

City of Blinks

They say it was organised in a peculiar way. It employed a system of government which never caught on, unique in history and fable. I'm grateful I wasn't born there instead of here, which is a utopia without the blinding flaw of the one I'm about to describe. Fetch something soft to sit on, unknown reader, and make yourself comfortable. If you pass this story on, be sure to include these instructions, and eventually we may have a world of adjusted cushions.

The city itself was constructed as a series of seven concentric circles, rising toward the centre like a perfectly round terraced mountain. In Atlantis today you may witness a similar design. The hub of this metropolis was a narrow cylinder taller than a mad king's ambition. On the very top he was perched, without a queen. Marriage would have ruined the schematic. Alone he watched his two chief viziers. In those days they came in pairs.

These viziers occupied the next terrace down, on opposite sides of the central circle. To keep them both in sight, the king was forced to sit sideways on his throne and view them from the corners of his eyes. Not easy, but this was simply one of the duties to be expected of a man in his position, so he didn't complain. Using this technique, he couldn't observe them carefully enough to describe their features, but he was able to tell whether they behaved themselves or not, and that was the important point.

The visual responsibilities of the viziers were of a less demanding quality, though more arduous in the sense of number. Each was required to watch four dukes on the third terrace from the middle. There were eight dukes in total and they were positioned on their circle at the main points of the compass. Whether they were dressed to represent the winds of those directions, I can't say. But neither vizier had to scan more than half a circle, which was sweet on their squints.

The dukes in turn spied on the next circle down, which held sixty four evenly spaced barons. The mathematical progression here is simple enough. The king watched two; the viziers four each, or eight in total; the dukes eight each, making sixty four; the barons sixteen each, making one thousand and twenty four judges, who were gathered on the fifth circle down; and they in turn each observed thirty two merchants, of which there were thirty two thousand seven hundred and sixty eight.

These merchants had little time in which to conduct their business, for they were charged with watching the artisans, the lowest social class, who suitably enough occupied the seventh circle, the one which formed the outer circumference of the city. Each merchant was obliged to watch sixty four artisans, so it's obvious that there were exactly two million ninety seven thousand one hundred and fifty two of those crafty swine, all level with the ground.

The sum population of the city was thus 2,131,019. Not one more, not one less. A network of suspicions. The circuit was closed in the following manner: the artisans all faced inward and gazed up at the king. Thus everybody came under scrutiny and no crime might be left undetected. In fact, with such a system of deterrence in place, the act of breaking a law, however minor, was unthinkable. The king was supreme. He genuinely was aware of every movement of all his subjects, not directly but through the web of visual surveillance.

And so the city remained alert. In this environment, the concept of revolution should have been beyond all hope. But in fact a revolution did occur, spontaneously, almost without the consent of the people, certainly without their prior knowledge, though once it happened they embraced it enthusiastically. It was a result of natural rhythms. As the king kept watch on his two immediate inferiors, he was compelled to blink at regular intervals. Despite his local omniscience, he was only human.

As the two viziers kept watch on the eight dukes, four each, twice the number watched by the king, because power and potential threat descended with title and status, they also frequently blinked. And as the dukes kept watch on the sixty four barons, eight each, twice the number watched by the viziers, they practised their own blinks. Which were almost identical to those of the barons who watched the one thousand and twenty four blinking judges, sixteen each, twice the number watched by the dukes. Needless to say, the merchants and artisans, despite their less refined expressions, cared not to miss out on this facial reflex. They blinked.

Each time this occurred, no matter which circle the culprit occupied, a tiny break in the pattern of total observation was caused. It hardly mattered, because the moment the blink was finished, the break was repaired. The system lurched onward despite these minor defects. They were flickering irritations, motes of dust in the eye of the process, but nothing more crippling than an itch which wanders the surface of the iris. And in common with many types of mild discomfort, the city grew numb to them.

Because none of the blinks were synchronised, the system held together, remaining more in the light than the dark, enduring as a viable tool of government. At any instant in time, the vast majority of citizens were being watched, and this was especially true of the king, upon whose distant central throne was trained an orbiting ring of more than two million spies. And here is the equation of his arrogance, for it takes that many artisans to equal one king, and more than thirty thousand merchants, over a thousand judges, sixty four barons and eight dukes, but only two viziers. No wonder he reserved a whole eye for each!

Anyway, over long periods coincidences are more common than unnecessary details and so it was inevitable that one day these polyrhythmic blinks would finally synchronise. Thus it happened. For a fraction of an instant, the city was blind. As every eyelid in the state closed together, the network shut down completely. Panic swelled in every breast, and mostly in the heart of the king, who felt helpless for the first time in his reign. What had happened to his personal cosmos? Had it vanished physically or was it merely divorced from his knowledge, and thus power, ready to continue without his input? And can an accident be accused of treason?

But his subjects were also lost without his beady guidance, his optic example. The viziers were visibly shaken, or would have been if any eye was open to behold their tremblings, and as for the remainder of this state's servants, all that should be said is that there was a symbolic cataract on the aristocracy and equally devastating metaphorical afflictions on the sight of the judiciary, traders and commoners. Take a dim view of these proceedings, reader, for they reveal how even the most perfectly sealed repressions can be undone in a blink of history.

Naturally all this political upheaval, the confusion, doubt, terror and twinge of social conscience, the latter a vague ache confined to the outer circle, only lasted an instant, for very soon the communal blink was over. A pair of eyes snapped open, then another and another, and the city was functional again, obsessively watchful, the eyelids flickering at varying speeds throughout the metropolis. But the old order didn't simply resume as if nothing had happened. The artisans were unused to the freedom that the momentary darkness had given them. For although they had all stopped watching the king, they too had not been watched, a disturbing and exciting fact, probably on the cusp of legality. They didn't know whether to feel ashamed or elated and so looked to their immediate superiors for a clue.

The merchants found themselves overwhelmed by this shifting of attention onto their own forms. They had no experience of being observed by quite so many eyes at once. The shared gaze of one thousand and twenty four judges was acceptable; but not the heaped glare of more than twenty million artisans, for the weight of this visual rearrangement was unbearable on their shoulders, movements and morals. No longer a fraction of a judicial eye on each merchant, but sixty four whole pairs! How heavy is an eye? The weight of a large grape? So a glass of wine pressing down on each forehead, a toast to scrutiny. The merchants were alarmed and outraged. They sought legal advice by turning their bodies and angling their heads up to stare at the judges.

Who were devoid of precedents for this situation and turned their own bodies and attentions toward the next highest circle, the domain of the barons, who also considered it best to follow suit and look at the dukes, all eight of whom silently appealed to the two viziers for advice by gazing at them, and the viziers, reluctant to issue orders on their own, at least not in such a strange crisis as this one, rotated slowly and awkwardly in their heavy robes and squinted up at the king. He was shocked by this development and having no higher authority to appeal to, stood up from his throne and surveyed the horizon of his rule: the artisans on the seventh circle.

So the circuit was reactivated but in reverse. Its polarity had flipped like a coin, even though this was before the notion of loose change. Indeed *change* there, especially political, tended to be no looser than a girl's bronze sandal worn by a giant. In other words, traditions were painfully fixed, and if one was ever replaced by a revolution, deliberate or not, the new custom would borrow all of its tenacity and much of its unfairness. But in this case the outcome was favourable to the majority, for it was the very first time an absolute tyrant was overthrown, or overlooked, by which I mean undervalued, by his citizens, or if you prefer, victims. The final result still wasn't a democracy, for that's a system where the ruling apex remains but is chosen by the masses. In this city, the hierarchy had been inverted. The king had become the *weakest* subject of his state.

He had lost all control, for whereas it was easy for the viziers to keep watch on him, and easier for the dukes to spy on the viziers, and even easier for the barons to examine the dukes, the judges to check on the barons and the merchants to peer at the judges, and *easiest* for the artisans to inspect the merchants, whereas all this was profoundly simple, I say again, it was extremely difficult, if not impossible, for the king to simultaneously stare at all the artisans. With more than two million to monitor with just two bleary eyes, it was as if he didn't exist. Such a large percentage of their actions escaped his attention that we might as well round it up to totality and declare them utterly free from being observed.

Free! What a hideous word for the king to contemplate. He believed he had constructed a political system that would last for the duration of all politics anywhere. Unfortunately the one thing not visible in his realm was its own weak spot, the possibility of a reversal of polarity. That is why his city never served as a true model for other governments. We are more sensible here, in our city. It too is constructed as a series of seven concentric circles, with a single king in the middle at the top, two viziers below, eight dukes, sixty four barons, and all the other numbers of judges, merchants and artisans. The circuit is the same. But our great tyrant will never be displaced by a function of physiology. *We* all spy on each other with organs which can't blink. For unlike eyes, ears are always open.

Herbert Quain, *Statements*, Vol 2, 1939

The Landscape Player

At first he played music on his instruments, reaching his audience through the purest melodies. His music washed over them, elevating them, burning their eyelids with tears or else trembling their lips with a dozen different kinds of smile. And when the vast wall of sound he had created had died away, there would be a silence more moving than any applause.

In time, he noticed that listeners were describing his music in terms of feelings. They spoke not of harmony and rhythm but of sadness and joy. They spoke not of keys and modes, but of elation and despair. The music was merely an interface. Accordingly, he started making instruments that played emotions instead of notes.

His scheme worked well; the critics were enraptured. His harps were threaded with heart-strings and plucked with plectrums made from the fingernails of dead lovers. His *Miserychords* and *Tromgroans* explored the outer limits of tragedy, a lugubrious drone agitated by the pounding *Kettle-Glums*, while on a different level, the *Mirthophone*, *Memory-Gongs* and rasp of the *Double-Bliss* provided a counterpoint of cautious hope and nostalgia.

The reviews were extremely favourable. People came from all over the land to hear him. But once again, they took refuge in metaphor. Now they spoke not of sadness and joy, elation and despair, but of a sea of tears dotted with misty islands, of evil vales of shadow and rosy mountains bathed in light, of dank gnarled forests webbed on mossy floors by a thousand cheerful babbling brooks. They explained their emotions in terms of landscape.

Deeply troubled and filled with rage, he took apart his instruments and reassembled them into something new. Now he could play landscapes.

In seven minutes he could play out his own Creation there on the stage, before them all. With his fingers on middle-sea and various salt flats, he stood them ankle deep in puddles where an angry sun had dried up a prehistoric ocean. Salt on their shoes, they kicked sand in a purple cloud, sliding across the desert toward a ruined amphitheatre*.

On and on they travelled, over the craggy sharps of unknown ranges that lacerated the sky. His brazen scales swung them in the balance; they ascended the crackling walls of icebergs and toppled over the other side. His miner chords took them deep beneath the Earth, under the drifting continents through a molten sea. And then, emerging from the depths of a volcano, they wove through a jungle of semi-quavers, trampled a tundra of tones.

The crashing crescendo became an enormous tidal wave bearing down on their heads, sweeping them onto the rolling steppes of the Coda. They suddenly realised that they were witnessing every sight that had ever existed and others that never would exist. They were exhausted, they were jaded. This was his revenge.

And yet, he had overlooked one detail. As he played the final chord, ready to storm off the stage, the final landscape shimmered into view. It was the landscape of the Concert Hall itself, complete with musician and instruments. He saw himself begin the piece afresh, from the overture. He guessed that he had condemned himself to an endless cycle of craters, sand dunes and rivers.

The audience grew restless. They yawned and fanned themselves. When he came around to the Jurassic again, most of them stood up and left. By the end of the last Ice Age, the auditorium was empty. He had tried too hard to connect directly with other people. He had forgotten that only in the act of love can the gap between desire and outcome be truly bridged.

Some say he is still there, multiplying himself forever, squeezing himself into the mouth of eternity like a snake that swallows its own tail, or like a raconteur who swallows his own tale. Others maintain that he has already

* He played the ruins of many lost cities, including Atlantis, Chaud-Mellé, Ambergris, Mirenburg and Viriconium, and it was impossible to say where one finished and the next began.

reached infinity and has been set free to play a penny-whistle on street-corners. Either way, it is generally agreed that, in the world of music, he managed to create something of a scene.

Fergus Hall, *The Young Person's Guide to Meaningless Parables*, 1975

The Spanish Cyclops

There was a lens-grinder who had fallen on hard times and who decided to revive his fortunes by exceeding the limits of his profession. Accordingly, he saved his remaining materials and set to work on the grandest project he could imagine.

The citizens of Valencia were perturbed at the noises which emanated from his workshop during the days and nights of a whole week.

At last he threw open his doors and rolled out into the town square the largest monocle in the world. It glittered below the green lamps which hung from the taverns and theatres. And soon a crowd gathered.

"What is the purpose of this object?" they wondered.

They walked around it, touching it lightly. It was too big to fit a king or bishop or even the statue of El Cid which loomed on the battlements of the palace. No eye in history might wear it comfortably in a squint. It was clear the lens-grinder had lost his sanity.

The soldiers came to lock him up in a madhouse, but he stalled them with an explanation. They rattled their pikes uneasily.

He said: "The entity for whom this monocle was made will seek it out when he learns of its existence. And he will pay me handsomely, because he has waited to see properly again for centuries."

There was much speculation as to the nature of this customer. People mounted the city walls to look out for him, but they saw nothing when they gazed inland. Once they called out that he was coming, yet it was only an elephant being led to a circus in Barcelona. Excitement and fear surged together.

While they watched, a ship from Cathay sailed into the bay and the citizens turned their attention out to sea. Even from this distance, the cargo of spices could be smelled. But as the vessel entered the harbour, a gigantic whirlpool opened up and sucked it down. The crew and all the pepper was destroyed.

A cry of horror filled the streets and bells were tolled in a hundred churches. Then someone remembered the great circular eyepiece and called out for help in rolling it down to the quayside. Within a minute, a crowd of volunteers were pushing at the rim of the monocle, bouncing it over the cobbles like a burning wheel.

The lens-grinder followed helplessly, tearing at his hair as his marvellous creation gathered speed. Soon it slipped out of the grasp of the thousand hands and trundled along a jetty and over the edge.

There was no splash. The monocle landed in the eye of the whirlpool, fitting it perfectly. Men and women rushed onto the jetty and peered over the side, gasping in wonder at what they beheld.

The ocean was no longer blind. As the whirlpool moved across the bay, it revealed the gardens of the deep. Through the sparkling lens it was possible to discern the seabed in astonishing clarity. And now all the wrecks of ages past were focussed on the surface, the gold and gems and casks of wine.

A few citizens jumped into boats and chased the roving eye to the horizon and beyond. They made maps as they did so, noting the position of each trove, planning for a future time when they might be hauled up and distributed equally among the population, or perhaps they were just enjoying the spectacle.

There was general rejoicing, but the lens-grinder went home in some trepidation and awaited a very big knock on his door.

Felipe Alfau, *Old Tales from Spain*, 1929

The Unsubtle Cages

Alone in a new city, the traveller decided to visit the zoo. It might be a place to find conversation, if not with people then with animals. He had not spoken for almost a week. He took a tram to the relevant suburb. The houses and factories were low and decayed. Dunes of rust drifted down the alleys, covering abandoned machinery. The wind was cold and constant. Newspapers from the previous century flapped across the wider streets, full of yellowing politics and adverts which could not be answered. They roosted with angry vibrations on the sagging telephone lines which conveyed static, sniggers and deep breathing from the hub of the metropolis to its rim. He had already come far but this short journey seemed much greater. An adventure.

He was the only passenger who dismounted outside the gates. They were neither closed nor open, but broken just enough to provide a means of entry. He climbed through. The zookeeper introduced himself. His name was Rotpier. He was not a malformed dwarf, but he acted as if he ought to be. He led the traveller past the compounds of lizards and worms. A few withered birds stood in groups on the tin roofs. Even Rotpier could not say whether they were part of the display or not. They were indeterminate. At last, the final cage was reached. It contained many other cages, all of different sizes. They stood idle, stacked in corners or on top of each other. They were worn and dented but perfectly serviceable.

"What is the meaning of this?" asked the traveller.

Rotpier blinked. "They have to be kept locked up for their own good. If they escaped, they might start caging beasts and people at random or according to their own tastes. Then they would return to the zoo with their new charges. The result would be an undisciplined collection, arbitrary and unplanned. Spontaneous, possibly automatic."

The traveller stroked his chin. "I wish to buy one."

"This is a very unusual request. I must consult my memory. Yes, I believe there is a precedent. Many years ago, a man called Belperron purchased a cage and took it back to his apartment, where he experimented on it. There are no laws against that. They are not expensive."

The traveller removed his wallet and counted out the notes. Then the zookeeper hooked one out with a long pole. It was heavy but responsive. It could be dragged or strapped to a back with equal inconvenience. Perhaps it might be rolled, in the manner of dice, end over end. The traveller left the zoo and waited for the tram with sore hands. It came and he paid a double fare. He sat opposite the cage, looking through its bars at the sombre view beyond the window. If the environment was trapped there, he must be free. The illusion comforted him to his destination. He pushed his new possession up the stairs of his hotel. He positioned it in the centre of the room. And this space which was not really his, this rented volume of continued existence, already resembled a new zoo. And he its keeper.

He waited for his first visitors.

It seemed an original method of defeating his isolation. His previous attempts to meet people had failed. The nightclubs were shut, the parks and subways deserted or unbearably strange. But now he had created a solution through the medium of business. Men and women would pay to tour his little zoo. They might bring children with them. Also laughter. It was almost feasible. He paced the floorboards for an hour before he realised that he needed a live exhibit to display in the cage. The answer was to lock himself inside. He would be fed and enjoyed until he achieved satisfaction. He did not swallow the key, but squatted over it. He removed his shoes and curled his toes. It was even more lonely in this simple cell, an outcome he had not anticipated. He licked his lips anxiously.

There was a rumbling from afar, as if a crowd was shuffling down the street toward his hotel. He imagined many outcomes. The authorities were coming to grant his zoo a licence or to close it down. The police were hurrying to arrest his prison and free him: a miscarriage of justice. He wondered why his cage did not return to the real zoo as Rotpier had predicted, with him as its trophy. The door of his room was closed. Possibly that was the reason. Or else it accepted the hotel as its home, validating the traveller's hopes. Then he imagined that the giant cage, the cage of cages, had detached itself from its location and was hunting its lost brother. He stood and gripped the bars facing the window. He was able to peer down onto the street. Rust dunes were shaken apart, settling evenly over the cobbles like the grains of a powdered sunset.

All his guesses were wrong. He saw rooms, dozens of them, sliding over this new desert, a caravan of cubes, misshapen, humped domiciles with grimy windows and flapping shutters like eyelids. Through each pane of glass, the unwashed outline of a traveller congealed. They were equally lonely, but the sum of all their feelings was still a single loneliness. One at a time, the rooms entered the hotel, passed through the lobby and up the stairs. He heard them in the corridor, squeezing between the walls. Now he felt the hotel swelling, an ego of brick and rotting joists and tattered curtains. The rooms were adding themselves to the collection. The symbolism was too obvious. He closed his eyes in the knowledge that each exhibit was its own visitor. And he experienced a relief so slight it bordered on monstrous despair.

Thomas Ligotti, *Confessions of a Medicated Lurker*, 1990

Celia the Impaler

The story of a woman who has made love to six of the Seven Wonders of the World, causing them to collapse from exhaustion, and how she attempts to seduce the seventh and last, the Great Pyramid of Cheops, unaware that it cannot fall down, because a pyramid exists in the shape of a building which has already fallen down. Told from the viewpoint of the capstone.

Silence is a threnody for she who cries in no dark; not tears but words, or the spaces between words. I have her now in the thirst of noon, lapping the shores of her knees, back arched painfully aware and heavy with dust. She is rigid but not as stone, tormented but not by fresh desire; her lusts are as old as any morning in a life. And yet high above the cold vapours of her shallows, mouth exhaling webs of breath, scent spiralling from skin and hair, I also watch.

She climbs higher along my crumbling limbs. The shimmer coils her neck; reality has its way with her peripheral vision. We recall in her graceful motion some aspect of our own reaching upward. Block upon block, grains hissing in mouth, a smile not for myself nor yet for you. Teeth not quite straight, yet not crooked; lips snarled in a chapped curl, tongue anticipating, fingers seeking. From heavy bliss to the moment of release, one pant exchanged for another, in a different key.

Down below, you are innocent enough, entranced by vendors, colours, the wailing of a dozen new guides. You have chosen not to follow; your wife is always playing such pranks, slipping out of your reach to explore the inaccessible. You do not even bother to follow her reclining figure with your eyes. You light a cigarette and rejoice in the small throat burn, the tiny blink. Up there it is for real.

The chance is beyond you now: the sun like a pool of ice is the screen. I wait with patience infinite as she picks her way towards the resolution I can provide. Already I have your secrets, your failures, revealed to me in the tension of her muscles. All the rage in her disappointment, known to all but yourself. They laugh, those who smile at you in the evenings, clustered around an empty bottle of useless wine. You are the spring of their indulgent wit; they almost love you for it. Almost kiss you.

Tell me, callow friend, what would you do if you knew the truth? Would you scramble up after her, chin held high, calling her name in impotent rebuke? Probably not. Chest too tight, heart too small, even down here. You sit on a smooth cube of rock and swelter, because you never swelter in the dirt. Besides, it is too late now: she is nearly at the top, where I linger as her lover, and her arms are clawing towards me. You are lost.

Let me remind you of that time in Rhodes, in Ephesus, in Babylon and the rest. They are the wonders; but for her there is only one source of wonder. The ache between her legs and how it is gouged free. Those others were mere flirtations; conjectures, the foreplay of possible sites, all flaccid from some earlier passion. Even then she asked you to come along, guessing that you would refuse. I am the consummation, the logical conclusion, the one remaining marvel.

Now she is up beside me, astride me, above me. I am a noble paramour and a deceitful one; I will take your wife's virginity for my own. Breathlessly, she hitches up her skirt and lowers herself onto my apex. The horns are yours, blistering youth, and you will never be able to justify your anger. The nuptial juice floods down my sides, slanting to the beds of sand all around, and her thighs glisten and undulate. Shall I reveal at last why I am the only one still standing, the seventh and best? No.

Michel Leiris, *The Rules of the Dawn*,
Headpress Books, 1927

Alone With a Longwinded Soul

A woman is sitting alone in a house. Perhaps her silence is like a pair of unused scissors leering at a tapestry, or a rocking chair without arms, back or scratch; it is an awful hush of suppression. Her stool does not scrape on the stone floor, for it is weighed down with a body so full of sadness that if her eyes burst, lobsters could scuttle up the ladder of her tears. But quietly, like a bell with a tongue for a clapper.

Her dwelling is narrow and tall and shaped like a nose which has never sneezed. If it runs it should be wiped on a cloud. The bricks are golden and the roof is blue, like a noon which has fallen through the sky. There is no ivy on the drainpipes. The windows are smudged with handprints, a record of her pressing engagement with flies. There is a verandah carved like a centipede with ninety stilts for legs. If it runs it should be tripped with a cat. Squat chimney, displeasure.

No need to peer over the landscape.

For the fields are red and busy with fat dust-devils which whip the dead trees until they bleed rust. And all the winds blow into themselves like this until the ground has sunk a full ten feet and the airy spirals are too laden to spin, whereupon they grind to a halt, obese and imperious, before collapsing again, spilling a billion grains over the exposed and tangled roots, like a statue or a mummy milled onto a giant cobweb. It is bleak but interesting out there...

And on the horizon the sun is bloated and poorly. It casseroles the moon in helium juices. These observations are truly unnecessary.

The woman never leaves her room, rarely her stool. There is no more point; she is the very last living thing. Her name is Thomasina Bailie Aldricha, and she knows she is alone in the whole world. How it happened: that should be a story! But it is not, for the process of destruction was so gradual, so inevitable, that a tongue which attempted to relate it would fossilise even in the abridgement.

There was a plan to save humanity, she remembers, but it was too clever to work. Like a skyscraper made of glass, it only revealed most of its upper flaws, even as it hoped to cut the heavens. A machine was constructed to block the deadly force which was falling onto the Earth; a device which drew its energy from the actual assault. Vast wheels turned above dying orchards. But these cosmic rays did not riddle, did not saturate, poison, stain. They sucked. They reeled. They travelled the wrong way, out into space, like hollow hooks on lines, snaring the continents, the seas, the heads, until the machine itself turned white, shook like a paper ladder and fell to fragments.

Thomasina survived because she had been a parasite all her life. Her husband had built her house, if not quite with his own hands then with his wallet, and she had lived in it to leech much more. He sat in the corner like a reluctant smile, growing smaller by the day, until it seemed he might squat in a jar instead. When his faith and bones were empty, she flicked a duster at him and he crumbled away. His love was like a sob on the far side of Saturn. Like a digested clock.

When a silver ray hooked her cheek, she was rummaging through his pockets, in trousers without legs. The two vampiric aspects, a pair of negatives, cancelled each other out, resulting in a positive. Her fingers were the modulus of her escape. She sighed and cooked a pan of beans on the spluttering stove. During his wake she slept. And because she always felt a meal was chewing her rather than the reverse, attributing her greed to it, the nourishment stayed with her. The rays understood. She lived and did not starve. Still she does not starve.

She is alone, the last, but so is the house. How the machine worked: a gabled tale! It was clear that human psychology was responsible for attracting the invasion. Acts of generosity were bait. Minds had to be distracted from virtue, suffused with an alternative, perhaps fear or anxiety. But no, this might be a lure for some other force. So a gentle nagging on the exact border of comfort and despair, between the two, a neutrality surely not appealing to any feaster on emotion. What rays could recognise such an ambiguity? Only those with nostrils on their wavelengths.

Every house in the world was assigned a number. Like a census of sand. Like all shaved monkeys finding their coats. Like no difference between words and thoughts. Then the stones or bricks or timbers or corrugated sheets of these dwellings were connected to the machine and the cogs were set in motion. A giant lottery wheel. For it chose a number, one every second at random, and destroyed the corresponding home. One domestic catastrophe a second. Sixty a minute. Three thousand six hundred an hour. Eighty six thousand four hundred a day. Six hundred and four thousand eight hundred a week. Thirty one million four hundred and forty nine thousand six hundred a year.

At first the people were frightened, waiting in their rooms for death, and this anguish did indeed invite a different set of rays to a banquet. But quickly humans realised they were much more likely to survive than be destroyed, that with forty billion homes on the planet, the process of complete demolition would take over a thousand years, nearly fifty generations. Time to live with no more worries than on any day before the implementation of the machine, yet with a vague feeling of unease which cheated the apocalypse.

But with the annihilation of each house, the odds were shortened. Although an individual's doom remained unlikely with every tick of the clock, it grew a fraction more tangible. A weight pressing on the mind, like a piano shedding keys in a kettle. The prices of houses next to those already smashed soared as people erroneously considered the law of chance to have ordained them as safer. For the majority, the panic returned, and they moved out of their homes into their gardens. So it was back to complacency and the rays.

When the machine broke, there was one number still left to pick. Thomasina's pile of bricks was last in the queue and never served with chaos.

She sits and debates whether to talk to herself. It is best not to, she concludes, for the world is unused to voices now and might shudder. If any lobsters were left they would climb. If any cats were left they might trip. If any other living thing was left it should know a fact, a lie, an idea, of some kind, any kind. Is this hope or is it not? Is this desire or is it not? Is it not or is it *not* not? Is it *is it not not* or is it *not is it not not*? A mouth might tell, but hers has fallen off.

Alone she rests, not waiting, for that implies culture. And it is all gone. Like a knife without a shadow, or a bag without a sigh. Like a pencil treated to a graphite display of violence. Like isolation in a bucket, or a mirage turning on a wheel. Like a whipped snake. Like a lamp kissing a lute. Like a lobster tripping over a cat. Like a shirt deceiving a cheese, or a catastrophic harmony. Like the shortest ghost story in the world extended by pretentious turns of phrase and unnecessary similes.

The doorbell rings.

D.F. Lewis, *The Weirdmonger's Tales*, Wyrd Press, 1994

Monkeybreath (halitosis simians)

Geographical Origin: the Spanish Main, 17th Century.
First Known Case: Pierre le Grand (Tortuga, 1602).
Last Known Case: Juanita Evita Zanahoria (Panama, 1671).

A condition limited almost entirely to real or pop. lit. pirates and their most dedicated imitators (excluding neighbourhood productions of faded musical comedies with obvious housewives posing as buccaneers and backdrop waves moved with crankshafts). Not a result of eating too much tropical fruit, as initially thought, but a consequence of prolonged swinging from rigging, bowsprits and mizzen masts, or over taffrails onto the decks of other vessels. The condition only attains full strength in conjunction with various other (implausible) factors, such as "Yo ho ho-ing!" and standing, exactly fifteen at a time, on a dead man's chest (see *Crush Injuries: Painful to Fatal* by J.G. Forcefeeble). Rum is an ineffective antidote. Private medical treatment for this disorder is not covered by insurance. A Piece of Eight (whatever that is) might be an acceptable unit of payment. Monkeybreath, and its most extreme symptom, the Great Yellow Mist, is unbearable in an individual. In a mob or crew, it is tempestuous, dangerous, useful.

The overwhelming odour of ripe bananas has been known to attract or discourage real apes and monkeys, depending on the latitude. A dramatic case concerns two rival crews of blood-and-grog-thirsty corsairs who were becalmed in the Antilles, parallel to each other, but out of cannon range, rather like a pair of indecisive political parties in the parliament of a long European country. To ease the frustration of not being able to engage each other in combat, the ruffian crews passed the time by practising various piratical (dastardly) customs: they tattooed themselves, spooned gunpowder into their daily grog, braided fuses in their beards, clenched knives between their teeth (*Take That Out Now Honey: Sharp Objects and Lacerated Tongues* by the Kansas-Kentucky Mom League), and of course swung from rigging, bowsprits and mizzen masts. The onset of acute Monkeybreath was inevitable. Suddenly, from the nearest island, just visible on the horizon, possibly Barbuda or Redonda, more than a hundred canoes were launched, each crammed with a selection of local primates. The canoes themselves were carved from giant mutant bananas! And paddled with huge banana leaves! Hitherto, only Zumboo, God of Monkeys, was reported to do that. And he was just a myth.

The pirates perceived the approach of this intimidating, gibbering fleet with extreme surprise and alarm, not to mention relief at having such a spectacle to distract them from their boredom. This combination of diverging emotions, each a supreme example of its kind, proved beyond the processing of facial expressions. Only the deepest sigh would suffice. The exhalation was communal and enormous. On both ships, the mainsails filled with the Great Yellow Mist. And now the perils (and advantages) of spooning gunpowder into daily grog rations became apparent, for this fog of elongated fruity essence was highly combustible. A loose spark from a braided fuse and JACKABOOM! the first pair of rocket-propelled galleons were shot out of a becalming in the Antilles, in opposite directions: like those rival political parties chasing the promise of bribes and prostitutes waiting at two separate exits of the parliament building. The surge capsized the canoes. Zumboo retains only a minor cult following in modern society.

Recently, a claim was made by an acrobat living in Curaçao that he had contracted the first case of Monkeybreath since the golden age of the buccaneers on the Spanish Main. Certainly his sighs smelled of bananas to an excessive degree. In sunlight he was prone to peeling. He liked to collect his breath in jars and post these, together with boxes of fuses, to a confidential address somewhere in Argentina. He repeated this behaviour at regular intervals, almost as if he was *trying too hard* to boost the velocity of a sailing vehicle on the pampas. Either he was mad or else he was suffering from sane lovesickness. Anyway, after detailed tests were conducted, it was determined that his halitosis was unrelated to historical (true) Monkeybreath but was merely a result of eating too much tropical fruit. Another disease with the same name is currently fashionable in certain parts of San Francisco, but is linked entirely with poor hygiene and dingy cinemas and is not contagious.

Dr J. MeerKat & Dr M. Rabbits, *The Thackery T. Lambshead Pocket Guide to Eccentric or Discredited Diseases*, 2003

Of Exactitude in Theology

...In that land, the art of Theology attained such perfection that to discuss even the smallest aspect of one of the gods took the study of a lifetime. It was thus decreed that the full nature of such gods was wholly beyond the understanding of man and that all metaphysics was therefore worthless. In the course of time, the college of Theologians continued to encourage further religious speculations with the sole aim of dismantling them as essentially inadequate. Succeeding generations came to judge such a system of dismantling in itself inadequate, and, not without irreverence, they dismantled it in turn. In the western deserts, a few dissolute scholars are still to be found, muttering an ontological proposition or two; in the whole nation, no other relic is left of the Discipline of Theology.

Jaromir Hladik, *A Vindication of Eternity*,
Book 4, Chap. 45, Prague, 1938

SURPLUS PARODIES

To Steve Redwood

Finding the Book of Sand

And all the sea were ink... — John Lyly

My name is Jazeps Zemzaris. I owe the present thirst on my tongue to my peculiar story. I owe my peculiar story to a book, a building and another book. The first book is the *Collected Fictions* of Jorge Luis Borges, published by Penguin Press in 1999 and translated by Andrew Hurley. The building is the Argentine National Library in Buenos Aires. The second book is impossible and should not exist.

After a life of regular and dreary work, I deserved to see a little of the world. This was my justification for buying an airline ticket to South America. But I could not alter my careful nature simply through an act of will, so of all the countries on that landmass I selected Argentina as my destination. It is the most European in character. To pass the hours of the flight more easily, I purchased a volume of short stories which also promised to introduce me to certain aspects of the culture of the nation I was visiting. This was the *Collected Fictions*. I read avidly in the sky. I landed in Buenos Aires and took a taxi ride through a city as beautiful as Paris, but I was eager to reach my hotel and continue reading. It was past midnight when I finished and switched off the light in my room. My dreams consisted of images from many of the tales. A story near the end held a particular fascination.

This piece was 'The Book of Sand' and it is about a man who collects books. One evening he is visited by a stranger who offers to sell him a tome bound in cloth. The collector is uninterested until the stranger tells him that this book has an infinite number of pages. If it is opened at random, the script that presents itself in an unreadable language will never be found again once it is closed. The collector haggles for the book and the visitor departs. He is pleased with his acquisition but in time it obsesses him. He decides to rid himself of it by carrying it to the National Library and losing it on a shelf in the basement, taking care not to note its position among the other books.

For me this story was a potent fable but one without a moral or with a moral I could not grasp. No doubt it would have faded in my memory as merely an example of clever writing, but a few days later on one of my excursions through the city I found myself on Mexico Street. I was seized by an impulse. When I entered the building I was surprised to discover it deserted. Nobody stopped me as I turned down the curved staircase to the basement. It was an hour before I found what I sought, wedged between Volume XLVI of a century old edition of *The Anglo-American Cyclopaedia* and *The God of the Labyrinth*, a detective novel by Herbert Quain, an author often recommended to me. I picked it out and held it to my chest until I caught my breath. Then I opened it. The truth tallied at every point with the story. The Book of Sand was mine and I was elated.

Until the day of my departure I grew increasingly concerned for the safety of my new possession. I felt no guilt at having liberated it, because infinity can rightfully belong to nobody or anybody. I concealed it at the bottom of my suitcase but I was still terrified it might be stolen. I became reluctant to leave my room. At last my vacation was over. I passed through Customs at the airport with a sweat on my face which fortunately resembled the juice of a fever rather than fear. At any rate I was not stopped. Back home I secured my doors and windows and experimented with the book. It did not disappoint. The script was unintelligible and augmented at two thousand page intervals by small illustrations of poor quality. Furthermore the numbering of the pages was arbitrary and no help in locating the beginning or end of the volume. Each time I attempted to find the first page by turning the cover I discovered that a number of other pages always came between the point I selected and the hypothetical flyleaf. The same applied to the last page. I closed the book and measured the width of its spine. Then I took a brush and ink and tried to paint a line across the edges of the leaves. The ink ran out almost immediately and no line was ever drawn. I wondered if the pages had absorbed the ink but I found no such stains at any point in the volume.

It was clear to me that this really was an infinite book. Unlike my predecessor in the story, I had a practical use for it. I am an engineer. I left my house with this prize concealed in a bag and walked to the abode of my former supervisor. The hour was late but he was still awake. He invited me in for a drink. He did not ask me about my trip, possibly because he has a distaste for polite conversation. Finishing my drink I reached into my bag and passed the book to him.

"Well Jazeps, what is this for?" he asked.

I said with a serious smile, "It's an infinite book. Go ahead and astound yourself with it. When you have accepted the truth, listen to me."

Coolly he replied, "I'm ready now."

"Very well. An infinite book can be read forever. But it is also a source of infinite fuel."

He tapped his nose. "I understand. We are hungry for energy."

I nodded. The power station had become ruinously expensive to run. In the story by Borges, the narrator toys with the idea of setting fire to the Book of Sand, but he fears it will burn forever and choke the world with smoke. I had no such worries. I knew that not *every* page could catch fire, because they were without limit. Only a finite number of pages would burn, an ever growing number that might be controlled by adjusting the amount of oxygen which reached the blaze. I also knew that the amount of smoke produced daily would be small compared to a multitude of other sources of pollution currently active. Besides, the hotter a fire, the more efficient it is and the less smoke created. The narrator of the story had missed a prime opportunity to contribute to the economy of his country.

That night my supervisor and myself designed a new power station from scratch. A sealed room lay at its core and at the centre of this unique blast furnace stood a titanium tripod upon which rested the Book of Sand. Above this was a water tank which was continually replenished from the local river. The burning book heated the water in this boiler to steam, which rose up a pipe at pressure and turned the vanes of a vast electricity generator. Most of this current ran into the national grid, providing power for homes and factories, but some was diverted to a number of large electric fans set into the walls of the furnace. These fed the fire with air from outside. As the number of burning pages continually increased, without in the least diminishing the infinite total by even one, and the water boiled faster and more furiously, so the pressure of the steam mounted, turning the generator faster and producing more electricity for the fans, which also accelerated the amount of oxygen they drew in. However, there was a limit to this process. When the fans reached their maximum speed, the blaze would stabilise. It would not increase in force indefinitely. And if there was a problem, the fans could be disabled, significantly reducing the amount of oxygen in the room and dampening the fire to a more manageable level.

My supervisor is an influential man. In conditions of great secrecy, the power station was constructed. Within six months of my return from Argentina, the majority of my neighbours were enjoying the benefits of free energy. Latvia is a small nation. A single perpetual motion machine, which in effect is what we had created, was more than enough to meet our power requirements. We prospered. I often walked around the perimeter of the clandestine station, nodding to the armed guards at the gate, imagining the scene inside the sealed room. I pictured the book as a ball of flame on its tripod, positioned directly under the vast boiler, raging in the artificial hurricanes of the spinning fans. The heat was surely intense and yet was maintained at a level below the melting point of the surrounding metal and brick. It was entirely safe. The drone of the fans reached me beyond the walls. The hum of the cables which extended overhead on pylons, channelling this impossible energy out toward the general population, was curiously like sacred chanting. The book itself was supposedly a religious tract. I recalled this fact from the story. Was it an act of obscure and possibly mathematical blasphemy to exploit it in this manner? And yet the number of remaining pages would always be infinite. Even if the book was cast into the sun and burned there until that star extinguished itself in untold future aeons, the total number of pages could not be reduced by a single unit. The rules of subtraction do not apply to infinity.

I should have experienced a profound happiness. But I was troubled and my sense of unease became steadily more acute. I began to regret my actions. I knew that the miracle of our power station could not be kept a secret forever. News of it would leak out. Other nations were sure to envy and admire our luck and ingenuity. In a short time our supply of free energy, the burning Book of Sand, would become one of the great clichés of our country. It would define Latvia as thoroughly and narrowly as the gaucho and the tango define Argentina. This in itself presented no problem. It was a minor irritation. But if the power failed for any reason, we would lose face. Our national pride would be critically damaged.

How could this happen? The danger lay in the possibility that the book was not infinite after all. The number of pages might be immense, even beyond calculation, but that is not the same as *infinite*. If indeed the book was simply a volume with a vast number of pages, rather than one with an endless supply, then one day it would burn out. The water in the boiler would cool and the generator stop turning. The more I pondered this idea, the more reasonable it seemed. There were three main reasons why I no longer believed the book to be infinite:

(1) The narrator in the original story made a list of the illustrations in the book, noting that they represented the objects of the real world and that no picture was ever repeated. He abandoned this project when his list became too long, but it must be pointed out that there is *not* an infinite number of objects in existence.

(2) The book is called the Book of Sand, apparently because *neither the book nor the sand has any beginning or end*. And yet the number of grains of sand in the world is finite. They can be counted, in theory at least, and one day a final total might be announced. A truly infinite book would surely bear some other name.

(3) An infinite book must contain an infinite number of pages. Each of these pages, however thin and delicate, must have *some* weight. An infinite book must be of infinite weight. I had not thought to weigh it when it was still in my possession and yet I knew for sure it was not infinitely heavy. I had lifted it from the library shelf and carried it back with me from the southern hemisphere to the northern.

These reasons compelled me to act. I had to sabotage the power station while it was still a secret and before it failed of its own accord. I was on friendly terms with the guards. Halfway between midnight and dawn of my chosen night, I approached the gate with several bottles of our national drink, *balzams*. As the bottles were passed around I took the smallest sips possible and yet the taste of orange peel, oak bark, wormwood, linden blossoms and alcohol burned my lips. I soon had the satisfaction of watching the guards fall into a drunken sleep at their posts. I went in search of the tongs I had hidden in the grass, found them and passed through the gate. I quickly disabled the fans and waited for the temperature inside the furnace to diminish to a relatively safe level before opening the door. The book still burned brightly on its tripod but with a reddish flame rather than a white one. Above it the boiler groaned as it cooled. My tongs were long enough to grasp the book while I stood on the threshold. I reversed out of the power station and turned around beyond the gates. Now I hurried through the industrial zones to the heart of the city.

My arms aching with my burden, I passed into the oldest quarter of Riga. The streets were deserted. I felt like the solitary member of a forgotten procession, my implausible torch passing the dark windows of many houses, reflecting from the glass in myriad flickers and multiplying the image of the infinite book. Now I carried the tongs over my shoulder and the book burned behind and above me like the knapsack of a wanderer in a new and unspecified fable. The narrow streets grew more crooked. I failed to notice the statuettes and carvings which adorn many of the buildings, because to me they are too familiar. I passed the cathedral with barely a glance. As I reached the Akmens Bridge, the streetlamps winked out. Much of Riga was left in darkness. The steam in the boiler was no longer forceful enough to turn the generator and was condensing back to lukewarm water. I felt suddenly conspicuous, like a firefly in the gloom. I crossed to the middle of the bridge and dropped the book over the side. It hissed as it struck the river. It went under and then resurfaced. No fire, however unbelievable, can burn without oxygen. I watched the book float away downstream. I did not know whether I had expected it to sink or not. I cast the tongs after it and they certainly slipped to the bottom. Then I went home in triumph to await my disgrace.

I was not imprisoned or sent into exile. I merely lost my friends and status. I moved to one of the poorer suburbs and lived alone, wasting my days in muted frustration, still partly believing I was a good man. Then the climate began to change. Gradually the level of the sea dropped. Ships ran aground as they approached ports. Every country in the world with a coastline found to its amazement that it was gaining territory. Eminent scientists were encouraged to devise theories which explained this phenomenon. None were convincing. Baffled geographers threw away their maps and globes. Only I understood what was happening. A normal book will absorb water until it is saturated, but a book of infinite pages will continue to absorb water until not a single drop remains. The Book of Sand had drifted down the river to the sea. Caught by currents it might have travelled thousands of miles before sinking. Now it lurked on the seabed somewhere, drinking water with an insatiable thirst. Eventually all the oceans of the world would be locked inside one book.

I imagined the sea draining away, revealing its secrets, the wrecked galleons and treasure chests and drowned mountain ranges. Locating the book and bringing it to the surface before all the water vanishes is unfeasible. Where to start searching? Only when there is no water left will it be easy to find. I thought at first the process might prove reversible. The sodden pages could be torn out and squeezed or the entire book pressed by powerful machines. But then I realised the futility of both schemes. The wet pages, however numerous, will be impossible to find among an infinite number, and compressing the book will simply force the liquid into other, dry regions of the volume, parched regions without limit. Once locked inside, the oceans are lost forever. The only water on the planet will remain in lakes and rivers, which must be damned at their mouths to stop them pouring away completely. A monumental thirst will be the worst thing to ever afflict humanity.

That thirst is already here. A submarine exploring the dwindling oceans last year reported entering a vast expanse of opaque water. Undersea storms have done nothing to break it up or dilute it. Larger and thicker it grows and now it has risen to the surface, spreading out like oil. It is black ink. The words in the Book of Sand have started to smudge and run. The unusual consistency of the ink means that it seals the water beneath it, preventing evaporation. Clouds are becoming rare. The planet is in the grip of a severe drought. Rain is only a memory. How will all this end? Will the oceans of water be entirely replaced by oceans of ink? Or will the book drink these also, reabsorbing what it has leaked?

I still dream of walking across a dry seabed, thousands of miles beneath a cloudless sky, and finding the book again. If I cast it into an active volcano will at least some of the water inside it turn to steam and pour forth to refresh the atmosphere and earth? There are too many possibilities. I have not yet considered them all. I tried to lose the book because I feared it was not infinite but the loss proved that it is. I have found irony, if nothing else. The beaches of the world no longer have tides to wash away the messages carved into the sand by lovers and children. The huge letters in many different languages stretch across untold millions of grains of sand, as my little life reaches across the greater number of pages of the book with that name.

The Hyperacusis of Chumbly Mucker

a parody of John Sladek in the style of a John Sladek parody

When the winds of the world were still fresh and people took breathing for granted, the child known as Chumbly Mucker was born in a large hospital. From the beginning, it was obvious he was different from everybody else. He suffered from extreme *hyperacusis*, an exaggerated sensitivity to sounds. This gift manifested itself in a singular and ultimately significant fashion.

So keen was his hearing that near sounds deafened him. Only distant noises were faint enough to be comprehensible. The rooms of the hospital were like cubes of solid thunder in which he was trapped, and all because a nurse was walking a corridor or a surgeon washing his hands. But a leaf gently falling in a deserted park in a foreign city was perfectly audible and agreeable.

His parents soon realised they could not communicate with their son by talking to him. Instead he learned language from remote sources. He became fluent in many tongues and always provided answers to questions other than those which had been asked. When visitors greeted him, he might offer one of the following replies:

"Me duelen los oídos."

"Ich mache es zum ersten Mal."

"Musím to projednat s našim predsedou."

"Benimle dansa gider misiniz?"

"Ana lastu jaahiz li-kull haaza."

And so forth. The visitors would frown and attribute his behaviour to flippancy, insanity or mere childishness. As he grew older, Chumbly remained unloved, except by his parents, who constantly devised schemes whereby they could hold a conversation with him. On one occasion they left him in the charge of an aunt and took a vacation abroad. No doubt they spoke to him successfully there, but by the time they returned the aunt had forgotten his responses.

One morning an elegant idea occurred to them. Moving to the telephone, they dialled the number of a friend on another continent. They spoke to this friend with words intended for Chumbly. The friend was bewildered but Chumbly listened, not to the voices which took it in turns to talk into the mouthpiece, for *they* were unintelligibly loud, but to the words which emerged from the telephone at the far end of the call. These words travelled back as tiny vibrations and reached his ears hours later, after his parents had retired to bed. He laughed in lonely darkness, for they had told him a joke.

They repeated this experiment on successive nights. In time they learned that the ears of their son were growing keener as he grew older. He was picking up conversations from countries on an ever widening circumference. Soon he would be listening exclusively to the antipodes. After that, what then? His parents were popular and had many foreign friends, but the time eventually came when they dialled the final number at the furthest point. They knew this would be the last conversation they could have with their son. It was poignant and awful. They hung up only when their friend was dangerously exhausted.

The following week, Chumbly spoke again. He said:

"Kay-ray-kuh-kuh-ko-kex."

His parents were in the habit of noting down his utterances and translating them with the aid of dictionaries and phrase books. But this one defeated them. A burning curiosity to understand it overwhelmed them. They sent a letter to the local university explaining their situation and quoting this strange outburst. A reply came sooner than they expected. There was a knock on the door and they opened it to discover a broad man with a false smile and slouched hat waiting on the threshold. He bowed slightly.

"The Muckers?" he asked and entered without permission.

"That's right. Who are you?"

The man hesitated. "Call me Doctor Word. I'm a top language expert. No, I'm not a *cunning* linguist. I'm more clever than that. I've read every phrase book ever printed. Now then, is that little Chumbly? See how he disports! Am I disturbing him? I would have made an appointment to see him next week, but your condition is urgent. May I remove my hat and request a cup of tea/coffee/chocolate?"

They rushed to comply and Doctor Word rested on the sofa. Chumbly played at his feet. It was a domestic scene made sinister by the academic ambience. The visitor rubbed his chin until his three beverages were ready and then he lowered his voice to a whisper which was undermined by the fact his arms made motions which attempted to convey the same information to a casual observer at the window, had there been one.

"An unknown language?" frowned the parents.

"I'm afraid so. We've tested the expression and discovered that it belongs to no *earthly* group. Clearly it originates from beyond this world. Outer space! From Venus/Mars or further, maybe even a planet orbiting a different star."

"But what does it mean?" they pressed.

Doctor Word shrugged. "We're not sure."

"And its significance? What about that?"

"Momentous. Truly. And not just because it proves the existence of extraterrestrial life. Sound, as you know, cannot travel through a vacuum. This suggests two astounding possibilities. (1) Outer space has an atmosphere. (2) The Earth is somehow connected to this other planet by a ventilation duct or alternative system of air-exchange. Clearly the first option is the least viable. Much better to gamble on the second. So we have."

"Who are 'we'?" demanded the Muckers.

"Myself and now you," said Doctor Word, "plus the higher agents of the university. Remember," he continued with a wink, "*you* contacted us."

This was true. There was nothing to be gained by complaining about any aspect of their visitor's news. They had to accept it without question, and take action, if that is what was required of them. So they nodded and meekly watched Doctor Word take polite sips from each of his drinks, which he never slurped.

Then they asked, "What shall we do now?"

"Ah, a most satisfactory attitude! This is a pleasant surprise. Ordinary citizens tend to be uncooperative. I hate defusing tensions because I only know one reliable method for doing so. It is forceful and dramatic."

He inverted the cups as he drained them and continued, "Since you are the parents of young Chumbly, it is only right you should be held partly responsible for whatever happens *because* of him. You must come with me."

Abruptly he stood and linked his arms with those of the Muckers, guiding them firmly but not inconsiderately toward the door.

"We can't leave Chumbly on his own!" they protested.

"Don't worry. He's safe. Note that I forget to retrieve my hat. It's an automated defence system which has been programmed to deal with intruders. The higher agents of the university employ many fashionable garments for this purpose."

Outside, on the small lawn, stood a helicopter. There was something not quite right about its appearance. Doctor Word ushered them inside, climbed into the pilot's seat and closed the hatch. They bounced across the grass and lurched into the sky, grazing the roofs of neighbouring houses. They clutched their stomachs.

"This is the Copterplane," explained Doctor Word, as he wrestled with the controls. "Although our agents never utilise disguises for our expressions, we deem it essential for our modes of transport. We are actually seated in an aeroplane. The cabin is fixed under a large circular wing, the lower surface of which acts as a screen for a hidden projector. An image of *spinning rotors* is thrown onto this screen to create the illusion of a helicopter."

"Ingenious!" croaked the Muckers.

"Yes, and look there!" chortled Doctor Word, nodding at a portion of the sky in which had appeared two bright specks. "Our escorts have arrived!"

The specks grew larger and revealed satisfying angles.

"That airship is really a helicopter hidden *inside* a bulbous frame which only seems full of helium. We call this device the Helizep. I guess you've already worked out that the aeroplane next to it is a disguised airship? Its wings are hollow and made of fabric. They *are* inflated, with helium or hydrogen, I forget which. That machine has no name yet. I want to call it Gladys, a suggestion that will be ignored, but it doesn't matter. The main thing is that observers on the ground will be tricked."

"What exactly are we looking for?" asked the Muckers.

"The ventilation duct which I mentioned as possibility (2). The search may be a long one. There is a selection of books in a compartment under your seat. They might help to ease the boredom. Only *one* is a work of fiction."

The Muckers groped for the volumes in question and studied the covers, failing to choose between them.

Hand Grenade Throwing as a College Sport, by Lewis Omer.
Wife Battering: A Systems Theory Approach, by Jean Giles-Sims.
Flying Machines in Disguise! by Dr Gaston Word.
Bohemian Life in Tenerife, London and Swansea, by Brigitte Fux.
European Spoons Before 1700, by John Emery.
Raising and Training the Parodist, by Duane Gardens, M.D.

Peering over the side, Doctor Word drew their attention to the fact they were above open country. The decaying wonders of the city had been left behind. That was good. Gentle hills raced their shadows up and down themselves. The Muckers breathed deeply, though the air in the cabin smelled of burning oil. Because they preferred to read the landscape to one of the books, Doctor Word banked the Copterplane to give them a better look. Ramshackle farms struggled along in the present economic climate.

"Look how tiny the sheep are! Just like lambs from up here!"

Doctor Word replied with a sneer, "There are no such things as lambs. The higher agents of the university have proved this thanks to a research grant. What you call 'lambs' are sheep which have shrunk in the rain. Because they are made of wool."

A little later he remarked, "We have agents everywhere. Even in the southern hemisphere. One of our finest was tragically lost forever in Buenos Aires. He got stuck in a hotel room and starved to death. An unfortunate accident. The DO NOT DISTURB sign was hanging from the inside handle of the door."

This story sounded oddly familiar to the Muckers. They guessed that Doctor Word was trying desperately to entertain them because he was scared. After all, *they* had brought the astonishing Chumbly into the world. Now their escorts made a different kind of sense. The phoney airship and aeroplane had drawn up close. After an hour, a range of mountains loomed on the horizon. The sun began to set in a typically beautiful manner. One of the Muckers raised an excited eyebrow.

"What's that? A vertical line in the sky!"

It was true. It seemed to have no top, rising higher and higher from a point just above the biggest mountain. They flew closer and circled it. A solid tube no thicker than an average finger. It was impossible to land on the summit of the peak or on the slopes, so they touched down on a glacier in the valley below and emerged from the cabins. The other two pilots were exactly like Doctor Word, but they had long beards and still wore their hats. They all commenced the climb up the mountain. Dusk settled on them. It was midnight by the time they reached their destination. The bottom end of the tube rested in the air just above the head of the tallest pilot, even though they were the same height. This was unnerving.

"We have located possibility (2)," said Doctor Word.

Stating the obvious was one of the few ways he knew how to relax. The Muckers decided to follow his example. They ironed flat the creases of their agitation with an exchange of hot blushes.

"You mean the interplanetary ventilation shaft which must exist as a *logical* consequence of Chumbly's recitation of the unknown word 'kay-ray-kuh-kuh-ko-kex'?"

Doctor Word looked grateful. "That's the one."

"Very impressive," they said, and so it was, with the stars as its destination, those twinkling distant suns happy in their arbitrary mythic patterns.

"What constellation is that?" they added.

"Canis Minor. The Lesser Dog. The tube appears to head in that direction. It's reasonable to conjecture it connects our world with another. Canis Minor does not lie on the *ecliptic*, which as any astronomer will tell you means this other planet orbits a different star. The tube must cross the gulfs of *interstellar* space!"

They considered carefully. "Remarkable!"

Doctor Word stretched out to touch the tube. "I can feel a slight suction. It's full of air. Obviously our atmosphere is being stolen, drawn off by an alien civilisation — drunk through a straw!"

He performed complex sums on his sinister and secret fingers. "The diameter of this tube is one centimetre. There are three significant stars in Canis Minor. The tube aims at the second brightest, *Beta Canis Minoris*, also known as Gomeisa, from the Arabic word 'al ghumaisa', which means 'the weeping one'. This star is 136 light years distant. One light year is approximately 10,000,000,000,000 km. So what is the total volume of the tube? Using the formula to calculate the volume of a cylinder, which is $\pi^2\perp$, we can estimate that more than *one thousand trillion* cubic kilometres of our atmosphere exists in that tube right now."

"Are you sure that's right?"

"Absolutely. And every breath of it stolen! It means that originally the atmosphere of our planet was much more extensive than it currently is. Perhaps it filled the whole solar system? But it has been drunk away over long ages almost to nothing. We are living in its dregs!"

He reached into a pocket. "This will foil their dastardly schemes!"

It was a book, but not one of the titles which the Muckers had examined. Doctor Word had sneakily reserved it for himself. He displayed the lettering on the spine.

The Pocket Universal Synopsis, revised by Julius Doppler.

He began tearing out pages, rolling them into pellets and stuffing them into the tube. They were drawn up with a horrible slurping noise. As he crammed, he spoke.

"If I had to write a book, another book I mean, I'd try to tell the story of Professor Fan, a colleague of mine. It's not a true story, fortunately. He was obsessed with the film actress, Phoebe Peng. Because he had influence at the university, he believed he might win her for real. He offered his *reputation* in exchange for a room in which he would be incarcerated with her for the remainder of his life. He specified that she had to be exactly as she was in her films. Somehow the transaction was made, but the wording of his demand went against him. He ended up imprisoned with a *perfectly flat* woman. She was like a shadow and only had one side. She slid up the walls and along the ceiling."

"Don't write it," advised the Muckers.

He nodded grimly and said, "The suction has stopped. I've thwarted our extrapolated enemies. I have saved the world!"

"Hurrah!" cried the two other agents, with strictly official enthusiasm.

They descended the mountain to the glacier, entered the flying machines and took off back to the city. Infrequently they looked over their shoulders at the retreating tube, so thin it was invisible and thus not worth observing. They sighed in amazement.

"The unknown word heard by Chumbly travelled all the way through its centre. It must have been spoken aeons ago."

Doctor Word licked his lips. "It was probably the very first word ever invented by that parasitical culture."

"Canis Minor! What are they like, we wonder?"

"Dog by name, dog by nature. That's implausible, but I favour it for reasons of verbal symmetry. They might have the bodies of men but the heads and tails of hounds. This reminds me of a startling fact. Dogs see everything in black and white! Exactly the same as old newsreels. They have no colour vision. Does this mean they lag behind in time? A recent research grant proved they do. Dogs are still living in the late 1920s."

"We're not academics," confessed the Muckers.

"No matter. You're almost home."

This was correct, but they were unable to land on the lawn in front of the house. The grass was already occupied by a large tent. The flag of the university fluttered above it. The Copterplane settled on a neighbour's lawn instead. The Helizep and provisional Gladys remained aloft. Doctor Word climbed out and beckoned for his passengers to follow. Before they reached the entrance of the tent, its flap parted and other agents emerged. Identical with hats.

"The house is protected. We cannot enter."

Doctor Word nodded. "I'll disarm my own hat. CHAPEAUX BAS!"

This shouted command did something to hidden circuits. Agents applauded thinly.

They said, "Thanks, but it doesn't matter. We set up a base here anyway. We have two pieces of news. First, our experts have deciphered the word 'kay-ray-kuh-kuh-ko-kex'. It's interesting semantically. It means whatever you *want* it to mean."

"That's useful," whistled Doctor Word.

"Second, average air-pressure everywhere is steadily increasing."

Doctor Word hummed. "This doesn't make too much sense. I have stopped it from steadily *decreasing*, but it should remain stable now. I'm dismayed actually."

"So you should be. If it continues to increase, every human being will be squashed flat — like a film actress."

"I bet this means there's another tube somewhere forcing air *into* our atmosphere. I'd better find it and block that one too!"

They gave him the university salute. A proud tear came to his eye.

He returned to the Copterplane with the Muckers. They ascended to search for the second tube. It might be anywhere, so that's where they went. Fields again and more mountains. Then the open sea. A storm was in progress. The lower part of this pipe was encrusted with salt. There was nothing to land on so he signalled to the other pilots to squash the tube flat between themselves to seal it. They collided from different directions and went down in flames. The stratagem worked. Huge waves extinguished burning fuel and lives. Doctor Word fled the catastrophic scene without sentiment.

"We deserve a relaxing vacation now," he said.

The Muckers nodded. "There has been a terrible mistake, hasn't there? Our atmosphere wasn't being drunk like a milkshake! For every cubic centimetre drawn off by the first tube, another replaced it through the second. It was a circulation system!"

Doctor Word hung his head in shame. The Copterplane veered crazily. "I admit it. I've inadvertently sabotaged some cosmic air purification machine. I'm sorry. The second tube appears to point at the star *Xi Puppis*, also called Azmidiske, meaning unclear. It is 1100 light years distant. Let's find a nice island upon which to have a barbecue."

They did so. White sands shimmered in the moonlight.

"What about Chumbly?" the Muckers demanded.

"Now my hat is disarmed, my colleagues may enter and feed him. But I feel the need to speculate awhile. I believe that every inhabited planet in the universe is connected to every other by a gigantic network of hollow tubes. One intake and one outflow pipe for each world. This is how our atmosphere is able to remain fresh. Otherwise it would go off."

"Already the wind is a bit stale."

Doctor Word sniffed. "I'm afraid you're right."

They began the barbecue, hoping the mingled odours of smoke and food would mask the sweaty scent of the breeze. Fetching a spare hat from the Copterplane, Doctor Word cast it into the sea. There were muffled explosions below. Dead fish washed ashore. The Muckers went to gather firewood. Although the whole experience was tropical, it was less magical than it should have been. It was like taking a holiday in a laundry basket. Doctor Word groaned.

"Clearly a planet is not large enough by itself to refresh its own atmosphere. This is something we didn't realise before. By blocking the tubes, we have closed down the entire system. The inhabited universe will eventually turn sour. And it's our fault!"

"Yours," corrected the Muckers. "Will engineers come to repair it?"

They glanced at the sky. It was a thought.

"I hope to high heaven it's insured!" they added.

"Eat up and I'll take you home. Everything has been ruined. I wonder how I might ever forgive myself? A research grant should allow me to discover the answer to that question. I'd better apply for one the instant I reach the university. Academic life has its hazards. I sometimes wish I was a simple human like yourselves. Or an innocent boy such as Chumbly. On second thoughts, he isn't so pure. Just mysterious."

"Amazing to think that all this happened simply because we had a child with very acute hearing!"

Doctor Word smiled patronisingly. "Don't worry. We were planning to mess up the universe anyway."

They cut short the sombre beach party and flew back to the city. The tent had vanished from their lawn. This did not mean the university agents had retreated, merely that they had decided to establish a permanent base and wanted to make room for the towers of reinforced concrete. They had probably gone to fetch building materials. Doctor Word waved the Muckers farewell and lurched away. He was low on fuel, but he would make it. They entered the house and found Chumbly playing with the hat. Breathing was no longer a pleasure.

"Not a fresh sniff of air to be had anywhere!"

Chumbly glanced up and said again, "Kay-ray-kuh-kuh-ko-kex."

"There! Did you hear that? Now we know the meaning of that word, we can deduce what he's saying when he uses it. And guess what? He's trying to tell us that he has thought of a way of sending information *faster than the speed of light*! What a prodigy! That's what the word means to us right now! The sealed tubes connect Earth with two other planets orbiting distant stars, right? These tubes are made of some futuristic (unknown) alloy and are thus rigid. It follows that if we rotate one at this end, it must rotate along its whole length. Its far end will rotate in perfect synchronisation with *this* end."

They contemplated some more and continued, "For instance, a quarter turn here will *instantaneously* be a quarter turn that end too! A simple code can be devised. A turn of so many degrees can represent a letter of a universal alphabet. We can transmit messages which they, whoever they are, will interpret! Messages explaining the situation about the stale air and appealing for help! But we can't do this on our own. We are laymen. If only Doctor Word hadn't returned to the university!"

Suddenly he was right there, under his hat.

He adjusted it to a jaunty angle and explained, "The hats of the higher agents are also radio transmitters and teleportation receivers. I had just reached campus when I heard your plea. Their range is limited but I arrived here pretty damned fast."

"That you did," they agreed affably.

He rubbed his palms together. "I like your idea. I've already dispatched agents to the locations of the tubes. They will devise your suggested code on the way."

"That's just dandy!" approved the Muckers.

"And when they get there, they will rotate the tubes between their fingers and thumbs."

The Muckers sighed with deep satisfaction. "What a revolution in the communications industry!"

"Yes," said Doctor Word. "If we fire a laser at either of those stars, it will take many years to reach its destination as the photons travel through empty space. But if those photons are already there, fixed along every instant of the distance in a *solid* beam, there's no empty space involved. In effect, this is what we have with those tubes."

Further explanations were unnecessary, so they sat quietly and waited. Secretly Doctor Word was planning the sorts of messages he would like to send himself. Requests, little flirtations, instructions for fabricating hats. A chance for the university to establish a colony through words. He regretted that the achievements of the higher agents had to go unrecognised by the general public. That was the deal. While he fretted, the Muckers frowned.

Finally they revealed what was on their minds. "We think Chumbly meant something *extra* when he spoke the word 'kay-ray-kuh-kuh-ko-kex' for the second time."

"Such as?" snapped Doctor Word.

"He was trying to warn us. Messages can now be transmitted instantaneously across thousands of light years. But nothing can exceed the speed of light according to the Laws of Relativity, which will adjust *anything* else — time, mass, etc — to maintain a constant speed of light. In this case, distance will be automatically adjusted. It will become much less."

"Oh dear," said Doctor Word. "They will be rotating the tubes about now..."

With an unimaginable sort of double flash, the alien stars suddenly appeared next to the Earth, one each side, vaporising the entire planet in seconds.

Ictus Purr

a parody of myself in the style of you

The tumbleweed that rolls through the streets of Swansea is unlike any other kind in any other place.

Most observers are of the opinion it isn't tumbleweed at all.

Optimists believe that abandoned beachballs have been shredded by the windborne sand into tangles of coloured ribbon and that they bounce past the crumbling houses and pubs in a fun way!

Pessimists suspect that clouds of oily fumes from the industrial complexes on the edge of the city have condensed into latticed globules of strange poisons and that the swirls of colour are due to impurities injurious to health!

For all anyone knows, they might both be right.

There's a restaurant called *The Chattery* and it sometimes lets bands play there, usually the soft kind, and it's a cosy venue with wine and candles. The sign on the door says CLOSED on both sides, but that's just a mistake. It's not really an elitist place but the smell of quiche is almost overpowering.

This night the place was throbbing with music which was bigger than the empty space inside. There's no stage, so the performers have to lurk near the entrance and play into the thickening shadows at the rear where the people who don't like music too much can attempt to hide. There was no escape from this particular band.

Maybe it was the twin fiddles or the baroque improvisations of the guitar or the tricky drum rhythms, or more likely a combination of all these elements, but whatever it was, a sort of aural weaving ended up producing a ball of sound with an exposed framework.

Sonic tumbleweed, that's what it was.

Great music certainly, but it had a shape which people expect to be left outside. There was a stirring among the audience. The odd thing, call it coincidence if you like, was that the songs had both beachy and industrial influences in them. So luckily and unluckily, the optimists and pessimists were both satisfied.

Later the band accepted a few bottles of free wine before packing up.

The five members sat at two tables, four together and one on his own. Let's consider the four first.

The lead singer was Neil Woollard and he spoke fluent Welsh. His hair was fluorescent. When the sun went down it flickered briefly and then shone with a steady yellow radiance. If he repeatedly put on and took off a hat he resembled a hazard light, the sort of thing that can hypnotise people.

The lead guitarist was Richard Cowell. Eighteen feet tall with an enormous stride, he seemed never to age. He always resembled a septuagenarian, but a very fit one. He grew the best marijuana in the region, acres and acres of it on a series of allotments, purely for personal consumption.

No taller than one of his knees, Kate Ronconi was a virtuoso who played instruments which nobody else had used for thousands of years. She found them in the tombs of ancient kings. Sometimes she played them all at the same time. She was fiery and possibly dangerous.

The fourth member was Huw Rees, brightly shirted, a man who lived with his drums as if they were pets, talking to them, feeding them, encouraging them to breed. His house smelled of tom-toms. His neighbours spied on him and chuckled in derision as they stroked their hatstands and lampshades*.

The loner at his own table was Hari Morgan, whose role was never to fit into any group, whatever their beliefs or aspirations. He once tried to join a guild of permanent outsiders but they wouldn't let him in. Or maybe they did let him in but he was so overqualified he passed right through and came out the other side, alone again. His chosen instrument was a crystal violin.

* Or flicked their beans.

Individually they were people. Together they were THE RAG FOUNDATION. Nobody knows how they came by this name. Optimists and pessimists have their theories, but we don't want to hear them. Do we? No.

The man who approached the band was dressed in a badly cut suit, or else the suit was perfect and he was in the wrong. He kept bowing as if he was on hidden springs but this was an illusion because the springs weren't hidden, they were attached to his joints on the outside, sewn onto the fabric. After they lost much of their force and he slowed down, the band noticed him.

"I sent the wine over," he said. "I'd like to talk with you."

"Our new album is available by mail order," responded Neil. There was a temporary fault in his hair, for it flickered rapidly, went blank, came back on a dull late horizon red.

"That's not it," babbled the man. "I want to book you for another gig. I'm a sort of talent scout. I used to track megatheriums but they went extinct. Now I seek and engage bands. My name is Jackfruit Bursts. I represent a syndicate of powerful critics."

"Speak to our manager," replied Richard.

"I can't do that. What I'm proposing must be kept quiet. I mean, the fewer people who know about it the better. The gig isn't in this universe. It'll be quite an adventure if you agree and I know you're keen on anything exciting and farfetched."

Kate reached across to fiddle with Neil's head, slapping it with her hand, shaking it, until his hair came on properly. "We don't sing about pirates anymore," she pointed out.

"We sing about whores instead," added Huw.

From his own table, Hari leaned across and whispered, "Autobiographical themes mostly. But fictional ones."

Jackfruit rubbed his chin, slightly surprised at this reaction, which was either more or less enthusiastic than he'd anticipated, he didn't know which. He paced up and down and licked his lips. He was acting nervou but it wasn't very convincing. Or else he was skillfully pretending to b unconvincing. He spread his hands wide.

"You'll get paid for it," he said.

Instantly the band were on their feet, spilling wine.

Jackfruit led them outside to his vehicle. At first they didn't believe he had one, but it was disguised as a giant tumbleweed. There wasn't a door. They had to enter by threading themselves through the filaments. A separate machine for Hari waited in its skeletal shadow.

As they accelerated down the main road, Jackfruit explained, "Best not to draw undue attention to ourselves. Blend in with the adjuncts of the environment, that's my guiding principle."

"We'll never get to another universe at this speed," grumbled Neil.

"You think not? Ho ho! But we won't leave the ground at any point other than for the occasional bounce, because we're not going into space. No, this craft is designed to slip between the dimensions."

"Ah, so it's a *parallel* universe we're headed for?" asked Richard.

Jackfruit nodded. "We won't need breathing equipment or radiation shields or parachutes. I'm grateful for this because they're rather expensive. Our route is lateral to the flow of time."

"It better not take long," warned Kate.

"I assure you it won't. I'm from that other universe and we are more technologically advanced than you. This vehicle is powered by an unexplainable generator! Yes it is."

They took him at his word and sat back to enjoy the scenery, which turned over and over around them. They didn't feel sick or if they did it was a sickness as mild as health, a background sickness always there and so never noticed, like the inner corners of a circle. Soon they were passing through a region of bizarre people with hollow faces who did disturbing things in outlandish clothes.

"This must be the point where the two universes meet," remarked Huw, "a sort of grey zone between the dimensions where the ordinary laws of physics and style are suspended. Look at the inhabitants of this eerie realm. They exist in a kind of limbo!"

Jackfruit shook his head. "We're still in Swansea. This is a street known as the Kingsway. It's always a bit dubious on the weekend. You won't feel anything when we pass over. That other universe is almost identical to this one. There are only a few differences."

"Such as?" inquired Neil, his hair going out again.

"Well, for a start, it has its own name."

"Universes have names?" gasped Richard.

Jackfruit chuckled at his innocence. "Naturally. I suppose if you've only ever lived in one you wouldn't know that. Names are only really necessary when there is two or more of something. The universe we are heading for is called Ictus Purr. Pass that joint, would you?"

"Ictus Purr! What does that mean?" asked Kate.

Jackfruit shrugged. "How should I know? It's the same with most names. They just are. Maybe they made sense as words in previous centuries but now they are usually just sounds. Ictus Purr is as good as Cupcake Boom, which is the name of *your* universe."

They mused on this for a minute.

"Tell us some names of other universes," urged Huw.

"As you wish. Mooseflake, Lust Basket, Blubberhack..."

His voice trailed away and Neil protested, "Don't stop! This is news to us."

"But we're almost at our destination now."

They peered out from between the struts and Richard scratched his head. "It looks exactly the same!"

"Not quite," returned Kate. "The lampposts and washing lines are odd."

"That's not enough to convince me," sneered Huw.

Jackfruit sighed. "Pay attention. I haven't turned around nor put my tumbleweed into reverse. I've kept going in a straight line. What's that building ahead?"

They peered at it carefully. It was *The Chattery*. But they hadn't gone in a loop. It was the same, but different.

Jackfruit smirked. "I'd better find somewhere to park. Nice hashish, by the way. Thanks."

Trailing behind, Hari took a wrong turn and ended up in a dimension which was ruled by two separate races who were engaged in perpetual warfare. One race had evolved from frogs, the other from barometers.

Weird landscapes ran with torrents of slime and mercury. Disembarking from his vehicle in the middle of a battlefield, Hari stubbed his toes on discarded weapons, warts and dials. He wandered about calling for his colleagues. Lilypads and isobars crunched underfoot. Unseen croakings and pressure differences mocked him.

Eventually he was captured by one side, escaped and was captured by the other. He learned the dominant languages and thanks to an unlikely set of circumstances managed to unite the two factions. He acted as the supreme leader for several years, exerting a civilising influence, teaching the inhabitants the meaning of such cultural delights as literature, art, philosophy, justice and surfing. He ordered the construction of windmills and shipyards. He told fables about impossible things such as giraffes and electricity. In return he learned much from them.

One day his people brought him an object they had discovered in a deserted place far beyond any habitation. They didn't know what it was and thought maybe he could work it out. Stepping down from his throne, Hari approached the enigmatic object and ran his hands over it. Then he climbed inside, wriggling his way to the centre, and steered it out of his palace. Without even a wave of farewell, he sped across the landscape, seeking the wrong turning he had made before. He finally found it. Years had passed for him but because of the paradoxes of transdimensional timeflow he arrived at his original destination just as the rest of the band finished setting up.

The amplifiers were humming and the audience was murmuring and the atmosphere was pretty much the same as in the other universe. But at least they were on tour. That's the way Neil, Richard and Kate looked at it. Nobody could say what Huw thought about the venue, least of all himself, because he was more concerned with softly crooning to his drums to calm their nerves. As for Hari, nobody asked for his opinion anyway. They didn't even notice he was late.

Jackfruit stood near the rear in the gloom, talking to his employers. They seemed pleased, though it was difficult to be certain because the shadows were very dense and few details of their expressions could be discerned. But they radiated a satisfaction. Beyond them lay blackness, utter and complete. Not the blackness of outer space, coffee or funk, but heavier and older than that. No light had *ever* shone into those depths.

"Our first gig in an alternative Swansea," said Neil. "It feels comfortable and yet exotic. Wrong and yet right."

The rest of the band didn't respond to this. He might be toying with new lyrics rather than talking to them. It was always difficult to tell. Jackfruit rejoined them and flustered about. He was excited and relieved. He asked the band to play directly into the shadows, over the heads of the audience if necessary. The tighter they played, the more they would be paid. Outside on the street, sand drifted in lazy patterns.

Richard asked, "Is there a parallel equivalent of my allotments near here? I'd love to visit them after the gig."

Jackfruit shook his head. "Sorry. In this dimension there are no open spaces, apart from the beach and a handful of small parks. I did say there were a few differences, didn't I? This version of Swansea covers the entire planet. The same buildings and coastline are stretched out around the globe. It is exquisitely horrible."

"But if what you told us earlier is correct," protested Kate, "the city shouldn't have a name, because there's only one."

There was despair in Jackfruit's voice. "If only that was true!"

Huw interrupted the conversation. "One of my snares has caught a cold. May I redefine the coughing as syncopation?"

The band nodded. "By all means."

Jackfruit clapped his hands. "Time to begin, I think. Shall I introduce you? I could say something like, 'Please welcome to *The Chattery*, all the way from Swansea on their first multiverse tour, one of the best new oldcomers in recent musical history, who now have several good albums to their name and have been practising their harmonies quite a bit, even though they no longer sing about pirates: THE RAG FOUNDATION!' Shall I do that? After all, you're new here even though you've played this venue before."

"Don't bother," said Neil.

"Is this the first of many such paradoxes?" wondered Richard.

Kate grimaced. "I'm not looking forward to playing a sequence of parallel Swanseas."

Huw nodded his agreement. "I was hoping to go further afield. Belgium, India, Cuba, maybe even Aberystwyth."

"Dream on," said Hari from somewhere ahead.

By now they had adopted their playing positions, settling into formation, and the feet of the audience began tapping in anticipation. Huw commenced a complex shuffle with his sticks and Richard strummed a few preliminary chords, jangly but somehow watery. Then Kate kicked in with her mediaeval hurdy-gurdy, Bronze Age harp and prehistoric *gnnuuurgh*! How she did this with only two arms still hasn't been properly researched. Finally Hari flexed his fingers over his violin and Neil opened the gates of his mouth to let out his thoughts in verbal form. The rhythms, harmonies and melodies were all multilayered and worthy of the prose of clever reviewers.

When they reached their last song, something unbelievable happened. Neil was a real performer and always liked to leap around the stage. Maybe the inhabitants of Ictus Purr were no less prone to spilling their wine than those of Cupcake Boom. Whatever the reason, he slipped on something and fell. He kept his back straight and toppled like a statue, but he didn't hit the ground. He came to a sudden halt at an angle of forty five degrees. Some sort of pole or strut kept him propped up.

The band stopped playing and blinked at him. He was still singing, probably as a reflex, and even without accompaniment he managed to hold the audience enthralled. Or maybe they were just unwell. The expressions can be remarkably similar. Anyway, his words came out of his mouth as a solid cylinder. It was this which had broken his fall. Where it touched the floor it spread out in thick ripples like a pool of oil, but it was constantly replenished from his throat. Solid sound.

In the dim light of the restaurant, this black cylinder wouldn't have been visible, but the jolt of his fall had reactivated his hair, which blazed forth like an indoor sun. It sent out rays which struck the crystal violin of Hari, who was standing just ahead of him. This transparent instrument acted like a prism and lens, bending and focussing the light to the rear of the venue. For the first time in eternity, its shadows were blown apart and all its secrets instantly exposed.

The open doors of an enormous hangar...

And inside the hangar: an artificial moon. A vast sphere, buttery and filigreed. You could look right through it.

There was a significant pause. Neil's song ended and the pole dissolved. He crashed to the ground and at the same time his hair burned itself out. Neon follicles are cheap to run but costly to replace. It was a shame, but there were higher priorities. Getting answers out of Jackfruit was the most important concern for the band at that moment. He didn't resist. He simply wound the springs on his clothes and shrugged.

"What's going on?" Neil spluttered.

Jackfruit replied, "Well, like I said, there are a few differences between this version of Swansea and yours. Three main differences to be precise. The first is that this city is much more stretched, which means every building is much longer and bigger than their equivalents in your universe. In Ictus Purr, *The Chattery* is large enough to contain a hangar and even a launch pad, for the giant ball actually rests on a colossal spring. The second difference is that sounds here have a tangible shape and substance."

"That explains why the lampposts look like quavers and the washing lines like musical staves!" gasped Richard.

"What's the third difference?" demanded Kate.

Jackfruit pointed upward. "Our sky doesn't have a moon! My employers are powerful critics, as I told you, but I didn't mention what they criticise. It isn't music! They are critics of the beach, which is littered with beachballs. To remove them more effectively we require a tide which will come in and float them away again. Without a moon we have no tide! I was sent to search the dimensions for a band who play tightly in a spherical shape. Eventually I found you!"

"But why bring us to this venue?" wondered Huw.

"Because it's dark and you couldn't see what you were creating. If you'd been too self-conscious, it might not have come out the same. Or you might have raised your fee. But it's finished and all that remains is to launch it into space and plaster over the gaps. I suppose we might even leave it with an exposed framework."

"Won't it fade away like an echo?" asked Neil.

"No, it's too memorable for that. The tunes you play tend to stick around. Lots of bands can make albums, but very few can make astronomical bodies of any gravitational importance."

"A tribute to our talent," said Richard.

"You don't think that creating a moon is a bit cheesy?" mused Kate.

"Not at all," answered Jackfruit and there was genuine conviction in his tone. He wasn't a propagandist for minor planets.

"May we watch the launch?" requested Huw.

"Of course! We might as well do it now. We're more technologically advanced than you, so we don't need a countdown. That's like you doing without an encore. It's a symptom of evolution. Stand back. It's a powerful spring! The manufacture of springs is one of our major underground industries. Would anyone like some wine? Whoops! There it goes already!"

They stood outside and bathed themselves in the light of a new moon. It felt self-indulgent but not decadent. The hour was late. The audience hadn't gone home but milled about on the street, postponing the return to bed. Everybody had an urge to hold hands, but they didn't. So it was an urge superfluous to future developments.

Jackfruit was the only one who gave in to his desires. He held his own hands behind his back and bestowed fond caresses on his fingers and thumbs. His earlier anxiety had vanished.

"You've done a big favour for this universe," he told the band. "I think the least we can do is repay it. Your audience are in no hurry to go home. I detect a unique opportunity."

"You want us to play another gig?" cried Neil.

"Yes, but not here. So few bands based in Swansea ever manage to play outside the city. Consider your own case. Even when you go on tour to another universe you end up back in Swansea! But now you have a chance to play at a magical new venue that is far away."

He pointed over the rooftops.

"On the surface of the moon?" spluttered Richard.

"Yes, or within it. That's your choice. What do you say?"

"How shall we get there?" wondered Kate.

Jackfruit pondered this problem. He replied, "Why not create a celestial ramp when the moon is low on the horizon? The gradient won't be too steep. Just play a sliding note. Sounds have substance here, remember? A long slow glissando on the *gnnuuurgh* should do it! Make sure you use a lot of reverberation. You don't want the ramp to fade under you and send you plummeting to your destruction!"

"Let's do it," roared Huw. "Where's Hari?"

They looked around. Hari had gone back inside. He was playing a solo into the empty shadows. His violin threw unglimpsed shapes into the darkness. The piece he played was obviously inspired by his frog-barometer experiences. It was uncanny and fabulous. He was building something back there but it was impossible to see what. The spring of the launch pad must have been wound automatically, for suddenly there was a mighty twang and an object rose into the sky to join the latticed sphere.

Hari emerged. "A separate moon for myself."

They nodded at his ingenuity. Then they squinted up at it. But it was much smaller than the first moon and no details could be discerned. Jackfruit reached into his pocket and drew out a microscope. He held this to one eye, closed the other and murmured.

"Here in Ictus Purr we don't use telescopes. Large distant objects look just like small near ones and that's the way we treat them! Microscopes are cheaper and less cumbersome. The difficult part is disregarding perspective. Well now! This extra moon looks like a white camper van."

"Surf's up!" explained Hari.

Jackfruit lowered the microscope. "I guess it is now." He laughed to himself as the two celestial objects approached each other. "Oh my! The new moon in the newer moon's arms! Make a wish."

The band did so.

It came true. They walked into the sky without falling back to the ground. They set up their equipment and played down into the city. As they sailed slowly from one horizon to the other they took the opportunity to try out some new songs. Pirates were still excluded.

Together they stroked the fur of the universe.

They are still playing, apparently.

The optimists and pessimists of Ictus Purr are agreed on one thing.

The musicians that play above the streets of Swansea are unlike any other kind in any other place.

IGNOBLE NOTES

Ignoble * Notes:

Preface to the Unpublished Edition

When I was very young, I assumed that the word 'infamous' meant *not famous* rather than renowned for being bad. References to the "infamous Marquis de Sade" confused me: I wondered how anybody might be well known for not being well known. In the whole of cultural history there are only two quotes concerning infamy and neither are true. The first comes from Macaulay: "The Chief Justice was rich, quiet and infamous." The second is from Kenneth Williams: "Infamy! Infamy! They've all got it *in for me*!"

Preface to an Imaginary Edition

Lunfardo is the slang used by the hoodlums of Old Buenos Aires. Borges' short story 'Streetcorner Man' (translated more accurately by Andrew Hurley as 'Man on Pink Corner') is written entirely in this colourful dialect. Typical Lunfardo expressions include the words 'leones', 'funyi', 'grela', 'canflia', 'quemera' and 'zurdo'. Wenglish is the slang used by the scoundrels of modern Glamorgan. Typical Wenglish expressions include the words 'twpsyn', 'belfago', 'bwci-bo', 'babilol', 'maldod' and 'ach-a-fi'. The two slangs have absolutely nothing in common.

* And ignorable.

The Brutal Buddha, Baron von Ungern-Sternberg

Grigory Semenov was one of the 'Atamans', informal leaders of the White cause who opposed the official counter-revolutionary forces as often as they resisted the Bolsheviks. Boris Annenkov, the most prominent Ataman, is credited with having created more Bolsheviks than he killed by treating the Siberian peasants with insufferable arrogance. More pragmatic than Annenkov, Semenov fled the victorious Red Army and went into exile in Manchuria, leaving less capable madmen to carry on the fight. Oddest of these was General A.P. Baksheev, who rallied peasants to the White cause by waving a fake Bolshevik flag, in the corner of which was stitched a tiny Imperial emblem. The conscripted soldiers would be sent to fight against Red Army troops, convinced they were attacking Whites. When Baksheev was captured and charged with underhand tactics, he justified his actions by claiming colour blindness.

Trader of Doom, Basil Zaharoff

An explorer as well as a painter, Nicholas Roerich travelled extensively in the remotest regions of China, Tibet and Siberia. In 1925, he embarked on a three-year expedition to find the 'lost' land of Shambhala. After many hardships, he chanced upon a wandering lama who explained that Shambhala was a metaphor for a higher mode of existence and thus not accessible to mortals. Roerich contented himself with depicting the ruined cities he had encountered on his journey. His brightly coloured canvases were an inspiration to H.P. Lovecraft who tried to capture some of their mystic grandeur in his novel *At the Mountains of Madness*. Roerich gave up looking for forgotten civilisations and settled in India, devoting himself to various humanitarian projects.

Streetcorner Mouse

Tin Dylan was responsible for writing some 3000 songs, none of which ever became famous or even infamous. However, one was adopted as the national anthem of the revivalists of the obscure island of Faskdhfgasdhia. The song consists of a two note drone and this single verse: "Necessity is the mother of invention / Despair is the mother of necessity / Stasis is the mother of despair / Boredom is the mother of stasis / Reality is the mother of boredom / Invention is the mother of reality."

Alone with a Longwinded Soul

This piece is a mildly surreal, wholly unnecessary expansion of a tale by Thomas Bailey Aldrich (1835-1907) which for many years was cited as the shortest ghost story ever written. The tale in question is called 'A Woman alone with Her Soul' and the full text runs: "A woman is sitting alone in a house. She knows she is alone in the whole world: every other living thing is dead. The doorbell rings." Falsely attributing the expansion to D.F. Lewis is appropriate, for Lewis has managed to write an even shorter ghost story than Aldrich. It is called 'I Might have Screamed Blue Rum' and consists of the single word "Murder." For several years I have been trying to understand the meaning of this tale.

Monkeybreath

One anonymous entry which was omitted from the final *Thackery T. Lambshead Guide* is a condition known as Tip-Top Shapies. The original text runs as follows:

"A particularly severe and uncultured form of Rude Health. It generally infects only those unfortunate, smug and handsome individuals who have adopted and maintained a rigorous and unnatural lifestyle. First they force themselves to abandon greasy foods and cigarettes. Secondly they cut down on beer. An urge to take regular exercise usually follows. Within a year, those who have survived the despair and ankle traumas (see *Foot in the Door: Careers at the Lower End of the Leg* by Dr Achilles Healer) have developed conspicuous signs of the illness. They are trimmer, faster, more supple in their movements, less prone to the common cold, less pallid about the cheek, more twinkly in the eye. Women love them, but I certainly don't. The loathsome bulges in their upper arms are ridiculous. Frankly, I have no desire to look like that. Besides, they are ignorant and uninformed, having little or no knowledge of current affairs, national or foreign, which is an obvious consequence of refusing to spend adequate time loafing in front of televised news broadcasts. Plus they have no sense of humour, because they also miss the cartoons. To be perfectly honest, I can't understand why those women like them so much. Perhaps they just feel pity? I know I do! It has been noted by sundry authorities that Tip-Top Shapies is the ideal disease of modern society. Like all true ideals, it is (or should be) universal. According to these sources, we are all sure to catch it 'sooner or later'. But anything that has to happen sooner or later won't happen NOW! So it will never happen. Because 'sooner' was about 10 years ago, and 'later' is approximately 10 years ahead in the future. Thus this disease has already been discredited, with the aid of my envy and ability to analyse glib common phrases. You can't get those from healthy eating and exercise. So there! (Anyone got a comfy chair?)"

Finding the Book of Sand

The narrator raises the intriguing idea that a book of infinite pages cast into the sun might burn there without being fully (or even partly) consumed. Indeed such a book would outlast the sun. However if it was cast into a star large enough to explode in a supernova (for instance Ras Algethi in the constellation Hercules) the spine and binding of the volume might be destroyed and ALL the individual pages blasted out into deep space. An infinite number of loose pages would completely fill the universe. The heavens would become solid paper and it would be theoretically possible to tear (and read) one's way between the planets, stars and galaxies.

The Hyperacusis of Chumbly Mucker

The rotation of rigid tubes across interstellar space would not actually transmit information faster than light, because a wave effect would still be involved as each molecule of the unknown alloy influenced the one next in line. Lacking academic credentials, the Muckers could not be expected to know this when they chose their particular interpretation of Chumbly's alien utterance, but Doctor Word and the other university agents should have known better — UNLESS THEY WERE FAKES. This suggests that the world was destroyed unnecessarily.

UNWISE APPENDIX
To Isabel Iglesias Valiño

Lönnrot avoided Scharlach's eyes. He looked at the trees and the sky subdivided into murky red, green and yellow rhombuses. He felt a chill, and an impersonal, almost anonymous sadness. The night was dark now; from the dusty garden there rose the pointless cry of a bird. For the last time, Lönnrot considered the problem of the symmetrical, periodic murders.

"There are three lines too many in your labyrinth," he said at last. "I know of a Greek labyrinth that is but one straight line. So many philosophers have been lost upon that line that a mere detective might be pardoned if he became lost as well. When you hunt me down in another avatar of our lives, Scharlach, I suggest that you fake (or commit) one crime at A, a second crime at B, eight kilometres from A, then a third crime at C, four kilometres from A and B and halfway between them. Then wait for me at D, two kilometres from A and C, once again halfway between them. Kill me at D, as you are about to kill me at Triste-le-Roy."

"The next time I kill you," Scharlach replied, "I promise you the labyrinth that consists of a single straight line that is invisible and endless."

He stepped back a few steps. Then, very carefully, he fired.

Jorge Luis Borges,
'Death and the Compass' (translated by Andrew Hurley)